STO

**FRIENDS
OF ACPL**

D1112517

THE ALICE AND JERRY BOOKS

READING FOUNDATION SERIES

FRIENDLY VILLAGE

MABEL O'DONNELL

Elementary Supervisor, Aurora, Illinois

ALICE CAREY

Formerly of the Lincoln School, Columbia University

Illustrated by
Florence and Margaret Hoopes

ROW, PETERSON AND COMPANY

NEW YORK CITY   EVANSTON, ILLINOIS   SAN FRANCISCO

Contents

STAY-AT-HOME STORIES

A FEELING IN YOUR BONES

MOUNTAIN STORIES

FIDDLE MUSIC

Copyright, 1941, 1936. Row, Peterson and Company 2077
Registered in U.S. Patent Office.   Printed in the U. S. A.
International and Imperial Copyright secured
All rights reserved for all countries, including the right of translation.

AUG 26 1944

CO. SCHOOLS
C166814

STAY-AT-HOME STORIES

Friendly Village

I know a village where you would like
to live. I would like to live there, too.

The streets run up hill and down hill,
and all the trees are big and beautiful.
The houses have a friendly look. There
are flowers growing in every garden.

A beautiful river runs through this village. Some of the houses are on one side of the river. Some of the houses are on the other side of the river.

The people who live on one side of the river go over to see the people who live on the other side. Everyone is as friendly as friendly can be.

Alice and Jerry live in Friendly Village.
Everyone knows Alice and Jerry.

Paddy lives in this village, and he likes
pets. Bobby and Billy live here, too. They
look just alike because they are twins.

Mr. Carl lives in Friendly Village. He has many birds in his white house because he likes to hear them sing. He hopes that someday he will have another bird called a nightingale.

Once upon a time Jack lived in Friendly Village, too. Then he moved to a farm in the country. But he likes his friends so well that he comes back again and again to see them.

One summer Paddy, Bobby, Billy, Jack, and Mr. Carl all went away. Alice and Jerry had to stay at home.

But exciting things can happen even if you do stay at home. And that summer exciting things did happen to Alice and Jerry. One exciting thing and then another!

Dolly Joins the Circus

Mr. Andrews Moves In

Summer days are long, long days, and many things can happen.

Alice and Jerry liked to have picnics in the woods. They liked to ride in Father's boat on the river. Some days they even went fishing.

But after you do the same things again and again, you wish that something new would happen.

That is why they were so happy when Mr. Andrews moved in, right next door. Mr. Andrews was their friend, you see. He was a friend to everyone in the village.

Mr. Andrews did two things to earn his living. He was the village milkman. In the early morning he took milk around to some of the houses.

After that he went to his fruit store on River Street. There he worked all day selling fruit.

Alice and Jerry had been to the fruit store many, many times. But they never thought that Mr. Andrews would come to live in the house next door.

When Mr. Andrews moved in, Dolly came, too. Dolly was his horse. She was old, but he liked her just the same.

Alice and Jerry thought there never was another horse like Dolly. She looked at you in the wisest way, and she was not afraid of anything.

Fun with Old Dolly

Dolly's white coat was gray in spots, and she was blind in one eye. Her good eye looked at you in a sleepy, friendly way.

Every morning when Mr. Andrews took the milk around to the houses, Dolly pulled the wagon for him.

After that she had very little to do. So she liked to stay by the garden gate near the big tree that grew there.

Alice and Jerry liked to climb up on the garden gate and then on Dolly's back. Dolly had such a good back to sit on. She had such a good back to ride on.

Dolly didn't care. She liked to have Alice and Jerry on her back. She liked to give them rides.

Up the street she would go and back again to the garden gate. Then Alice and Jerry would climb off, safe and sound.

The Circus Comes to Town

One morning Mr. Andrews walked out to his barn. He put his hands in his pockets and looked up at a big circus picture on the side of the barn.

The picture was so big that it took up all one side of the barn. It showed all the circus animals. It showed an old clown, too, as funny as funny could be.

Right at the top in big letters, it said,

STREETER'S CIRCUS
THE BIGGEST SHOW IN THE WORLD

Mr. Andrews was still looking up at the picture when Alice and Jerry came out of the house. He called to them as soon as he saw them.

3 1833 02926 6282

"I suppose you are happy today," he said. "The circus is coming to town. Come, see the funny old clown."

But Alice and Jerry were not happy. They did not want to look at the clown.

Just a few days before, Father had handed Jerry his spending money and Alice her spending money.

"Do not forget," Father had said, "the circus is coming to town. Put your money away if you want to go."

Jerry wanted to go to the circus. But the next day he saw a baseball in a store window. It was just the ball he had wanted for a long time. When he went into the store, he forgot all about the circus. It took all Jerry's money to get that ball.

Alice wanted to go to the circus, too, but she did like ice cream. She got some one day and some more the next. Before long her money was all gone, too.

Now Circus Day was here, and Alice and Jerry had no money for tickets.

Of course, they had to tell Mr. Andrews how it all happened. And, of course, Mr. Andrews did his best to make them forget about the circus.

"Come now," he said, "you just stay here with old Dolly. She is not much like a circus horse, and she must have a new shoe, but—"

Before Mr. Andrews could say another word, Jerry pulled his arm and danced up and down.

"We can ride her. We did once before. We can ride her down. Please, please, Mr. Andrews! We can take old Dolly to get her shoe."

Mr. Andrews really did not have time to take Dolly to the blacksmith shop just then. He really wanted to go right down to his store on River Street.

"That is a long way for you to go alone," he said.

"Mother will not care," said Jerry. "We ride old Dolly every day. We can take her. Please, Mr. Andrews, please!"

The end of it all was that before long Alice and Jerry were on old Dolly's back going right down the street to the blacksmith shop.

Now there were two ways to go to the blacksmith shop. One way did not take long. The other way took much longer and went right down River Street.

Alice and Jerry chose the longer way.

Dolly Joins the Parade

Dolly walked along with Alice and Jerry on her back. She had just come to the church on River Street when she stopped.

She had heard something. It was music —music that Dolly had not heard for years and years and years.

Alice and Jerry heard the music, too. They knew at once what it was. It was the circus parade.

As Dolly stopped, her head went up. Her ears went up, too. She did not look like an old horse now.

Then all at once Dolly started to trot. Faster and faster she went right down River Street.

Alice cried, "She is running away! She is running away!"

But Dolly was not running away. She was not acting like a runaway horse. She was acting like a horse that knew just where she wanted to go and was going to get there as soon as she could.

"Hold on, Alice! Hold on!" cried Jerry again and again.

The music came nearer and nearer. Dolly trotted faster and faster. Nothing could stop her.

Then up River Street came the parade.

Before Alice and Jerry knew what had happened, they were in the parade, too.

A big circus wagon was in front of them. Behind them was a dancing clown. His painted face was as funny as funny could be.

Now Dolly began to walk. But what a step she had! Head up, she stepped right in time with the music. You could tell she had been in a parade before.

How everyone did laugh and shout to see them!

But Dolly stepped right on. She was in the parade, and there she was going to stay. Nothing could stop her.

All Alice and Jerry could do was sit on Dolly's back and stay in the parade, too.

Up and then down River Street went the parade, right by all the stores. Of course, it went right by Mr. Andrews' store.

Mr. Andrews stood in the door of his store. What was this he saw? Dolly in a circus parade! How did she get there? Where was she going?

But before Mr. Andrews could do a thing about it, the parade had moved on. Not even he could stop the parade and get Dolly out.

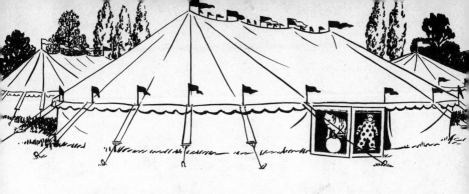

The Old Circus Horse

The parade went on down the street and out of town. There, just outside of town, were all the circus tents.

Right into the long horse-tent trotted old Dolly with all the other horses.

Alice and Jerry got down from Dolly's back. No one looked at them. Everyone looked at Dolly.

"An old circus horse! That is what she is! Did you see the way she stepped in time with the music?" said one of the circus men.

"When I started to work for the circus, we had a horse like that," said another man. "She is a circus horse all right."

"She is not a circus horse," said Jerry. "She is Dolly. She is Mr. Andrews' horse, and she pulls the milk wagon for him every morning."

"Well, well!" said one of the circus men. "Here are the boy and girl who rode old Dolly."

"How would you like some good seats for the show?" said another man. "Here are two good seats for two good riders."

He gave Alice and Jerry the tickets. How surprised and delighted they were!

Just at that minute Mr. Andrews came running into the tent. He was looking for Alice, Jerry, and Dolly.

"We are going to the circus after all," shouted Alice and Jerry. "Look, Mr. Andrews, look! We have two tickets for the circus."

Then they ran right by Mr. Andrews and out of the tent. They had to run home to tell the good news to Mother.

In the Big Tent

It looked as if all the people in town were in the big circus tent that afternoon. And right down on the front seats sat Alice and Jerry. All the circus people knew them as soon as they saw them.

Many, many things went on in the tent that afternoon, and Alice and Jerry saw almost everything.

When the circus animals walked around for the last time, Alice pulled Jerry's arm.

"Look!" she cried. "There is Dolly!"

Yes, it was Dolly, but Dolly as she had never looked before. Her white coat looked beautiful, and the gray spots did not show. She had a new shoe. She did not look old now. On her back rode a beautiful circus lady.

Dolly Joins the Circus

That night Dolly joined the circus. When the circus went away, Dolly went, too.

"We can not have a circus horse pulling a milk wagon," said all the circus men. "We will take good care of Dolly."

With the money Mr. Andrews got for Dolly, he bought an old car to carry his milk bottles.

Many times when the car would not go, Mr. Andrews thought of Dolly and wished she had not joined the circus.

"When the circus comes next year, Dolly will come back, too," said Alice.

And do you know? When the circus came the next year, there was old Dolly.

The Old Barn

Mr. Andrews' Day Off

Did your mother and father ever have some old thing that they did not know what to do with? It was something that was still good—too good to throw away.

If you had a barn at your house, I just know that is where they put it.

But if people put old things in a barn, year after year, there comes a time when something has to be done about it.

The people who had lived in the house before Mr. Andrews moved in had put old things into the barn until it was so full that it would hold no more. When they moved away, they left all the old things behind them. They took everything from the house and forgot all about the barn.

What was Mr. Andrews going to do? Really, he did not know. That is why he stood one morning with his hands in his pockets and looked and looked at that old barn.

"I will have to take a day off from my work and clean that barn," said Mr. Andrews. "Even one day will not be enough."

The next day Mr. Andrews got someone to stay in his fruit store. He started early in the morning to clean that barn. He threw out the first things he came to, basket after basket of bottles and cans.

He made so much noise that Alice and Jerry heard him. Soon they were out of bed and right down at the barn door ready to help.

It took twenty minutes to get out all the bottles and cans. Then they started on the next things they came to. Tables and chairs, pictures and beds followed one another out of that barn.

"Put them over here," said Mr. Andrews. "I will sell them if I can or give them away to anyone who wants them."

I can not take time to tell you all the things they took out of that barn. But I will tell you that Alice and Jerry and Mr. Andrews worked all day.

By the time the sun went down, that barn was clean, even to the windows.

Just as they were ready to go home, Alice looked up.

"Oh, Mr. Andrews," she said, "there is another story to this barn."

And sure enough, right over their heads was a hole that opened up into the second story of that barn.

"Yes," said Mr. Andrews, "but we have worked enough for one day."

The Ladder in the Barn

One morning Alice was looking for Jerry. First she looked in the barn. There she saw a ladder going right up through the hole to the second story.

"Mr. Andrews! Jerry!" she called, but there was no one in the barn.

Then Alice started right up that ladder. By the time she had climbed a few steps, she wished someone were there to catch her if she fell.

So she came down the ladder and ran out of the barn to look for Jerry.

There was Jerry in Mr. Carl's garden looking for worms. He was going fishing.

"Oh, Jerry!" she called. "There is a ladder in the barn. Did you see it?"

"Don't talk to me about barns now," said Jerry. "I am going fishing."

"Yes, but don't you want to climb the ladder?" asked Alice.

"Not until I get this can full of worms," said Jerry.

Now, there was nothing in the world Alice liked less than worms. She did not like to look at them. She did not like to put them into a can.

But if Jerry had to have that can full before he would climb the ladder, she knew she had to help a little.

Every time she put a worm into the can, a shiver went right up and down her back. It was surprising how many worms that can did hold. And all the time she went right on saying over and over again,

"Come on, Jerry! Come on and go!"

At last, when the can was just about full, Jerry stopped.

"That will do for today," he said. "I am not going fishing until tomorrow anyway. Come on, Alice! I will go now."

The Surprise in the Barn

Alice knew why Jerry put off fishing until tomorrow. He wanted to know what was in the second story of the barn, too.

Soon they were in the barn.

As Jerry started up the ladder, he said, "There won't be anything up here but truck, Alice—just truck."

In just a minute Alice could hear him walking around over her head.

"Alice! Alice! Come on up! Come on up! There is something up here," he called.

Up the ladder went Alice. She did not stop this time to think how far down it was to the ground, or how far up it was to the second story. She just went.

And there, leaning right up against the window, was a bicycle—a very old bicycle with just one wheel.

"Oh, dear! Oh, dear!" said Alice. "It is just good-for-nothing."

"Maybe we can find the wheel," said Jerry. "Come on and look, Alice! Come on!"

They pulled out all the truck they could move, and they climbed over all the rest. But they could not find that wheel.

Then at last up through the hole came Mr. Andrews. How surprised he was to see Alice and Jerry!

Of course he said they could have the bicycle, and of course he started right in to look, too. But not even Mr. Andrews could find that wheel.

Alice and Mr. Andrews thought they might just as well give up looking. But not Jerry—he would not give up.

At last away back in a dark corner Jerry saw the wheel.

"Do you think you can put it on? Do you, Mr. Andrews? Do you?" cried Jerry.

"We will hope for the best," said Mr. Andrews, and he started down the ladder with the bicycle.

Jerry followed with the wheel. Alice came right down after them, and no one had to help her.

Then Mr. Andrews started to work. Alice and Jerry stood right by his side every minute to see just what he did.

It was very hard to make the wheel stay on the old bicycle so that it would be safe for Alice and Jerry to ride. But at last Mr. Andrews did it. He always did what he started out to do.

And then, of course, you know what happened.

"Hop on, Alice, and I will hold you," said Mr. Andrews.

First Alice had a ride, and then Jerry had a ride. Then they had rides all over again. Oh, how much fun they had!

When the next day came, Jerry forgot all about fishing. All that day and the next and the next, Alice and Jerry rode and rode and rode. CO. SCHOOLS C166814

No one could count the times they fell off. But they did not care. They just picked themselves up and started all over again. My, but they had fun!

How happy they were when at last they could ride right down the street to Mr. Andrews' store!

Jerry could ride without holding on. Alice could not do that. She just rang the bell—ting-a-ling, ting-a-ling—to tell people to get out of the way.

And they all did get out of her way. "That old bicycle may fall to pieces any day," they said. But it never did.

All summer long Alice and Jerry rode the old bicycle through the streets of Friendly Village. Everyone laughed when he heard them coming. That old bicycle made so much noise!

"What would we ever do without it!" said Alice again and again.

"We just could not get along without it," said Jerry. "It was a lucky day for us when we climbed that ladder."

Now if there is someone near your house who has been storing things in his barn for a long, long time, suppose you go over someday and help him clean it out. It will be good for the barn, and maybe you will find something, too—something that will be just as much fun as the old bicycle that Alice and Jerry found.

FEELING IN YOUR BONES

 # Seven O'Clock in the Morning

One, two, three, four, five, six, seven! It was seven o'clock in the morning as Jerry jumped out of bed.

In a few minutes he had on his old shoes and his old blue overalls. He had a big smile on his face and he looked as if he were all ready for a good day's fun.

"Oh, Mother!" he called. "I am so happy and I don't know why. Something exciting is going to happen. I can feel it in my bones."

Father liked to say he could feel things in his bones. So Jerry liked to say it, too.

Mother was getting breakfast for Jerry.

"Well, you never can tell," called Mother from the kitchen. "Some days are like that. But if something exciting is going to happen, it will happen to you alone. I have so much to do this morning that Alice is going to help me."

When you have a feeling in your bones, it never takes long to eat your breakfast. In a minute or two Jerry stood at the back door, thinking what he was going to do next.

And then—believe it or not—something exciting did happen!

Right down the road and into Mr. Andrews' garden trotted a white goat. He started in right away to eat the sunflowers that grew at the corner of the old red barn.

Jerry looked once. He looked a second time. He could not believe his eyes.

A goat in Mr. Andrews' garden! Mr. Andrews did not have a goat. No one in the village had a goat. Where in the world had he come from? Anyway, he must stop eating sunflowers.

"Get out! Get out!" shouted Jerry, as he ran down the steps.

Now, I suppose the goat wanted to get out when he heard Jerry shout.

But there was only one way out of that
garden. That way was through the garden
gate. Jerry was coming in at the gate
right at that very minute.

How could the goat get out? He could
not. So he took one more sunflower and
started to go some place. He really didn't
know where.

Round the barn went the goat, and
round the barn after him went Jerry.
Round and round! Round and round!

Then all at once Jerry missed his step. Down he went, but not for long. He picked himself up and started after the goat faster than ever.

He went round the barn one way. He went round the barn the other.

But look where he would, the goat was nowhere to be found. In the garden — in the barn — down the street — no goat!

This was surprising! There had been a goat here. Jerry was sure that there had.

He ran home to tell Mother.

"Why, Jerry," she said, "you must have been seeing things."

Jerry was sure he had not been seeing things. Look! The sunflowers were all gone. Where in the world had that goat come from? Where in the world had he gone?

Eight O'Clock in the Morning

There is something about a summer morning that makes you want to take your time doing things. You feel like doing the things you want to do and forgetting about the others.

Mrs. Hill should have cleaned her kitchen. She should have made the beds. She should have done all her housework.

But she just took a look around and went out to work in her flower garden.

When you have the best flower garden in town, you like to work in it. Mrs. Hill liked it so well that she did not look up from her work. It is too bad she didn't.

If she had looked up, she would have seen something white going right down her outside cellar steps.

All was still for a time. Mrs. Hill went right on working.

Then all at once there was such a noise in that cellar. It sounded as if all the milk bottles, all the fruit cans—everything in the cellar—were falling to pieces.

In less than a minute, Mrs. Hill was going down the cellar steps, too.

As she ran, she saw something white through the cellar window. She could not believe her eyes. It looked very much like a goat.

"Get out! Get out!" she shouted all the way down the cellar steps.

Now, I suppose the goat wanted to get out when he heard Mrs. Hill shout. But he could not get out the way he came in. How could he? Mrs. Hill was coming down the steps. But he had to go some place. So he took the other way out and went right up the inside steps to the kitchen.

Now, I told you Mrs. Hill should have cleaned her kitchen. If she had put things away, there would not have been so much for that goat to upset.

He started in by upsetting a few chairs. By the time Mrs. Hill got to the kitchen, he had upset the table and everything on it.

She threw open the door, shouting, "Get out! Get out!"

"M-a-a-a! M-a-a-a!" said the goat, and out he went.

Mrs. Hill picked up just one chair. Then she was out of the door after the goat as fast as she could go.

But look where she would, the goat was nowhere to be found. In the garden — around the house — up the road — no goat!

This was surprising! There had been a goat here not five minutes before. Mrs. Hill was sure that there had. Where in the world had he come from? Where in the world had he gone?

She ran over to tell Mrs. Gray, who lived next door.

When Mrs. Gray heard about the goat, she said, "That is a good story, but there has not been a goat in this village for years and years and years!"

"But there is a goat here now," said Mrs. Hill. "Come and see my kitchen."

Then Mrs. Gray went home with Mrs. Hill. They stood for a minute and looked at that kitchen. Then they forgot it was a summer morning and cleaned and cleaned and cleaned.

Ten O'Clock in the Morning

When you live in a village, you can be very sure you will have good things to eat, for the farms and the country are not far away.

Almost every summer morning Alice and Jerry could see the farmers coming to town with good things to sell.

If the farmers had fruit to sell, they always stopped at Mr. Andrews' store. He always bought some fruit, you see.

There was a farmer in front of Mr. Andrews' store this morning with a wagon full of apples.

Mr. Andrews was there, too, with his coat off and his hands in his pockets, talking away to the old farmer.

"You won't find worms in my apples," the farmer was saying.

"They are the best apples I have ever seen," said Mr. Andrews. "They will be just the things to put in my front window."

"I will have something to show people when they come into my store today," Mr. Andrews went on. "Give me six baskets."

Just at that minute the man who had the store next to Mr. Andrews' came running up.

"Show people!" he said. "You have something to show people right now. He just ran in your back door."

Mr. Andrews did not know what the man was talking about. So he turned to look at his store. There through the front window he saw something white. It looked very much like a goat. He could not believe his eyes.

It did not take Mr. Andrews a minute to get back into his store. But the goat had upset all the fruit in the place.

"Get out! Get out!" shouted Mr. Andrews.

Now, I suppose the goat wanted to get out when he heard Mr. Andrews shout. I suppose he wanted to go out the way he came in. But Mr. Andrews was so cross that the goat was all turned around. He thought the front door was the back door.

"M-a-a-a! M-a-a-a!" he said, and out he went.

The old farm horse was right in front of the door. He was not blind in one eye like Dolly. But it was a good many years since that horse had run.

He ran now. Up went his ears and down River Street he went, with apples flying everywhere.

The old farmer shouted, "Hold on, there! Hold on! Hold on!"

Everyone looked at the runaway horse, even Mr. Andrews. When the horse stopped running, Mr. Andrews thought of the goat.

But look where he would, the goat was nowhere to be found. Up the street—down the street—in front of stores—behind the stores—no goat! This was surprising!

There had been a goat here not five minutes before. Mr. Andrews knew that there had. Where in the world had he come from? Where in the world had he gone?

Is There a Goat? Yes. No.

So it went on all morning long. Here
and there, here and there, all over the
village, that goat showed up—first in one
place and then in another. He upset things
and made mischief wherever he went.

And all the people who saw the goat
believed in him. As for the others—well
—they just smiled and said, "Why! there
has not been a goat in this village for
years and years and years."

Yes! There Is a Goat!

You know that sleepy time that comes in the afternoon on a summer day?

Mother's work is done at last and she wants to take a nap. She thinks it is too warm for you to go outdoors. It is too warm to play baseball. She wants you to stay in the house and be still.

Jerry's mother was just like that. When she went to take her nap that afternoon, she said, "Now, Jerry! You have been running around all morning looking for that goat. Please rest for just ten minutes."

Jerry wanted to please Mother. So he took a chair by the front window and began to look at some pictures.

They were circus pictures—pictures of the big tent and all the circus animals. Some of the pictures showed funny clowns climbing up ladders, riding on bicycles, throwing balls, and dancing to music.

Maybe Jerry would have sat still for ten minutes and looked at the pictures if his friend, Bill, had not come down the road, shouting at the top of his voice, "Jerry, Jerry! I found the goat!"

No one—not even Mother—would have wanted Jerry to sit still after that news. Anyway, he didn't.

"Where? Where?" he shouted, as he ran out of the house.

"Down on River Street! Down on River Street! Come and see!"

How Jerry and Bill did run!

When they got to River Street, they saw a crowd—a crowd that was getting bigger and bigger every minute.

And all the people on the outside of the crowd were laughing.

But all the people on the inside of the crowd were cross—very cross. They were all talking as fast as they could talk, and all together.

And right in the very middle was a little, round, fat man. He looked as if he were made to be jolly. But, of course, he was not jolly now. There were too many cross people talking to him.

And there in front of him, all ready to pull a gay little wagon with red wheels, was a goat—a goat that stood with his head down looking at the ground.

The goat was acting as if he never could get into mischief—no, never!

"I tell you he did get into my cellar," said Mrs. Hill. "He upset all my fruit cans. You should have seen my kitchen by the time I got him out. It gives me shivers to think of it."

"Lady! Lady! It was not my goat. He is a good goat. He stayed with me all morning. He was eating grass."

"Eating grass? No, he was not!" said Mr. Andrews. "He was in my fruit store. That is where he was. He upset all the fruit in the place."

"Yes, and he ate all your sunflowers, Mr. Andrews," called Jerry.

"What?" said Mr. Andrews. "I didn't know about that."

Then all the other people who had seen the goat that morning told their stories of the mischief he had been into.

And all the time the man with the goat looked as if he wanted to get away —out of town—any place away from there.

Now you know how it is when you get cross. After you have said everything you have to say, you feel better. After you feel better, some of the things that made you cross seem very, very funny.

This was a lucky thing for the man with the goat.

All at once Mrs. Hill remembered how surprised she had been to see a goat through her cellar window. She started to laugh and she laughed until she cried.

Mr. Andrews remembered the runaway horse and the flying apples. He had to tell everyone about that.

The more he told, the more he laughed, until he had to hold his sides, he laughed so hard and so long.

All the other people—even the cross ones—joined in.

By this time the man with the goat began to look jolly—just the way he was supposed to look.

And the goat—well—he looked up and all around. There was mischief in his eye and—believe it or not—I think he laughed, too.

Then Mr. Andrews said to the man, "Where in the world did you come from? What are you doing in this village?"

Where Did He Come From?

"I give boys and girls a ride in my wagon for ten cents," said the man. "I take their pictures for ten cents more.

"We walk from village to village, my goat and I. But sometimes the road is long and we are very tired. This morning it was warm on the river bank so I found a good place to take a nap. I left my goat to eat grass, but he must have run away."

"I should say he did!" said Jerry. "He ran all over the village."

"Yes," said the man, and he looked as if he could not understand. "But when my nap was over, my goat was still eating."

"Well, you see," said Mr. Andrews, "your nap was not a nap at all. It was a good long sleep. That goat had time to get into mischief and eat grass, too."

And I believe Mr. Andrews was right, don't you?

The End of It All

The end of it all was that every boy and girl in Friendly Village had a ride in that gay little wagon with the red wheels— all for nothing.

"I will make up for all the mischief my goat has done," said the jolly fat man.

When the boys and girls heard the good news, they were very happy. But it was not good news for the goat.

Every boy and girl had a ride to the blacksmith shop and back again.

At first the man walked by the side of the wagon. But before long the goat could go and come back all by himself.

Then all the boys and girls who had ten cents for spending money had the man take their pictures.

It is a good thing it was a village and not a town or city or that goat might have been giving rides to this very minute.

It was almost five o'clock in the afternoon when the rides were over—over at last— and how tired the goat did look!

"We must get to the next town before dark," said the jolly fat man.

So the man and the goat started on their way. And really—I don't think that goat ever wanted to come back again.

Then Jerry and Mr. Andrews started for home all by themselves. Jerry had a picture of himself and the goat, and he thought it was beautiful—yes, just beautiful!

"All in all," said Mr. Andrews, as they rode along in his old car, "this has been an exciting day. Nothing like this has happened in Friendly Village since the day when Dolly joined the circus."

"You are right," said Jerry. "But then— I knew something exciting was going to happen. I told Mother so this morning. You see, Mr. Andrews, I can always tell when exciting things are going to happen. I can feel it in my bones."

In the Mountains

Do you know what mountains really are? If you live in the mountains, of course you know. But if you have never seen the mountains, suppose you look at this picture.

It is lovely in the mountains in the summertime! Here all the world is still and beautiful. Up and down the mountain-sides are the deep pine woods.

Here and there you can see the brown log cabins. Trails go from cabin to cabin and up, up, up over the mountaintop. Grass and mountain flowers grow in the open places.

It is lovely in the mountains in the summertime.

Pig-a-Wee

A Mountain Pig

Away up on the side of a mountain there lived a little pig. Her name was Pig-a-wee, and she was all full of hills and hollows just like her own mountain country.

Lem, the boy who owned the pig, lived in a little brown log cabin. The cabin stood in an open place in the woods.

Of course, Lem's father and mother lived in the brown log cabin, too.

It was a long, long walk down the mountain trail to the next log cabin, and sometimes Lem and his mother and father were very lonesome.

"If only we had a tune box," said Mother.

"Yes," said Lem, "a beautiful tune box with a horn like a big morning-glory. Then we could have music all day long."

"Why not take Pig-a-wee and go down to the store in the village," said Father. "Maybe you can sell Pig-a-wee for a tune box."

"I will go right away and see," said Lem.

So up over the mountain and down on the other side went Lem with a rope around Pig-a-wee's leg.

Down, down the mountain went the trail, right by Granny May's cabin! Down, down, and around the mountain and right by Preacher Day's cabin! Down through the deep pine woods until at last Lem came to the store in the village!

"Would you take my pig for that beautiful tune box?" Lem asked the man in the store.

"Oh my, no!" said the man. "That pig is much too skinny. She is nothing but bones. But I will take a cow."

"Oh dear, no!" said Lem. "Father would never give you the cow. She gives us milk every day."

"Then I will take two pigs," said the man.

"But we have only one pig," said Lem. "How can I give you two?"

"Then I will take four piglets," said the man.

"But we have no piglets at all," said Lem.

There was nothing left to do but go home. So Lem took Pig-a-wee and started up the mountain trail. The rope was still around Pig-a-wee's leg.

Home Again

They had not gone far when Pig-a-wee pulled away from Lem. She went up the trail so fast that Lem could not catch her.

So Lem climbed up the mountain all alone. He was feeling very tired.

It was not long before he heard a noise, and there was Pig-a-wee right in the middle of Preacher Day's melon patch.

"Gobble up my melons, will you? You good-for-nothing pig!" shouted Preacher Day.

He ran round and round after Pig-a-wee. All at once Pig-a-wee bumped against Preacher Day's legs and upset him. Some of the melons rolled away down the mountainside.

Pig-a-wee ran under the fence and away so fast that Lem and Preacher Day could not catch her.

So Lem climbed up and around the mountain all alone.

Then all at once he heard a noise again, and there was Pig-a-wee right in the middle of Granny May's potato patch.

"Eat up all my potatoes, will you? You good-for-nothing pig!" said Granny, and she ran after Pig-a-wee, round and round the potato patch.

"Wee, wee, wee!" cried Pig-a-wee, and she jumped right through the fence and almost got away.

But this time Lem got hold of the rope around Pig-a-wee's leg, and she could not get away.

After a long, long climb Lem and Pig-a-wee came to the top of the mountain, and there, down on the other side, sat their own little cabin.

Smoke was coming out of the chimney. Lem could smell the good things Mother was getting ready for him to eat.

"Wee, wee, wee!" cried Pig-a-wee when she smelled the good smell, too.

She pulled away from Lem and ran down the mountain so fast that she missed her step. Over and over she rolled right down the mountainside.

I really believe she must have rolled right down the chimney because Mother, who was working in the kitchen, heard a noise of something falling down, down, down.

She turned around to the fireplace, and there was Pig-a-wee. The pots and pans were flying everywhere!

"What, are you back again, you good-for-nothing pig!" cried Mother.

"Wee, wee, wee!" cried Pig-a-wee. She jumped through the door and upset Lem on the doorstep.

Lem picked himself up and walked into the kitchen, looking very tired.

"I can see that you did not get the tune box," said Mother.

"No," said Lem. "The man in the store wants four piglets for his tune box. Pig-a-wee is too skinny for him."

"Then she is good-for-nothing," said Mother. "Tomorrow you must take her into the woods and leave her there with the other wild pigs. She must root for herself from this time on."

The Tune Box

The next morning Lem took Pig-a-wee into the woods and left her there.

But Pig-a-wee was his own little pig, and Lem was very, very lonesome.

So every morning and every night Lem went out to the woods to see Pig-a-wee. He always had something for her to eat.

Lem always found Pig-a-wee at the edge of the woods looking for him.

But one morning Pig-a-wee was not to be seen. The next day and the next, it was the same way—no Pig-a-wee.

Lem wondered and wondered where she could be. At last he started into the woods to find her.

It was not long before he found Pig-a-wee—and four little piglets.

"Mother! Father! Come and see!" shouted Lem, as he ran back to the cabin. "Pig-a-wee has four little piglets."

Mother and Father came running.

"Wee, wee, wee!" cried Pig-a-wee proudly. "Wee, wee, wee, wee!" cried the four little piglets all together.

"Now we can get the tune box," cried Mother and Father and Lem.

When the piglets were big enough, Lem took them down the long mountain trail to the store in the village.

"Here are the four piglets," he said. "Now may I have that fine tune box?"

"Yes, of course you may," said the man.

So Lem took the tune box and started up the trail.

Preacher Day sat on his doorstep.

"See what I bought with Pig-a-wee's little piglets," called Lem, and he played a tune for Preacher Day.

On Lem climbed until he came to Granny May's cabin.

"See what I bought with Pig-a-wee's little piglets," called Lem, and he played a tune for Granny.

Then on Lem went up and up and over the mountaintop. Down on the other side was his own little cabin.

Mother and Father were looking for him. "Here he comes," they cried when they saw Lem on the mountaintop. They could hardly wait to hear the tune box play.

They played one tune and then another, and every tune was better than the one before.

The next day Preacher Day and Granny
and crowds of people from up and down
the mountain came to hear the tune box
play. Everyone had a basket of good things
for Pig-a-wee.

"What a wonderful Pig-a-wee she is!" cried all the mountain people when they heard the tunes come out of the morning-glory horn.

Pig-a-wee was very happy. I believe she ate about twenty melons, and seven or eight baskets of potatoes, and twenty-five ears of corn.

Maybe you do not believe this, but that is what someone told me. Anyway, she gobbled and gobbled. But even then, she could not eat up all the good things the mountain people had for her.

The Blueberry Pie

Work to Do

It was early one morning just after breakfast. Almost all the housework was done because Mother was going up the mountain to see her friend, Mrs. Pool.

Father had gone down the mountain to the village to sell pine wood.

Lem was going to stay at home and get pine wood for the fireplace and give the cow and Pig-a-wee some breakfast.

And because he was going to do this all by himself, Mother had made him a pie—a blueberry pie with a little hole in the middle of it where the juice had come through. There was the pie right on the table looking at him.

Now there was nothing Lem liked to eat so much as blueberry pie. He thought he was very lucky to have a big pie all for himself.

There was one more thing for Mother to do before she went up the mountain. She took out her big brown bowl and started to make some corn bread for Lem's dinner.

Lem came over and looked into the bowl.

"M-m-m-m!" he said. "You know what I like, Mother. Corn bread and blueberry pie! M-m-m-m!"

When Lem thought of the good dinner he was going to have, he whistled a gay, mountain tune.

Lem's yellow pup was asleep on the doorstep outside. He heard the whistle and gave one jump through the open door.

But as he jumped, he bumped into Mother. The bowl flew right out of her hands and was broken all to pieces. The corn bread went flying all over the floor.

"Bow-wow!" said the yellow pup, when he saw the mischief he had done.

"Oh, my bowl—my brown bowl," cried Mother. "It is the only bowl in the house. What will I do without it?"

"It is all my fault, Mother," Lem cried. "I whistled and that is why the yellow pup ran into you."

"Now don't think anything more about it," said Mother. "Things like that will happen sometimes. I still have time to clean the floor."

"I will clean the floor, Mother," said Lem. "I can do it. Really I can."

"Very well," said Mother, "but you will have no bread for your dinner, Lem. I should take time to make some more."

"There is blueberry pie," said Lem, looking at it where it sat on the table. "Maybe I could have two pieces all at once, and that could be my dinner."

"It is not a rich pie," said Mother. "You may have two pieces. You may have even more than that if you are hungry. It is your own pie, but take care— don't eat too much."

"I won't," said Lem. "I will be sure about that."

Mother put the things she was taking to Mrs. Pool in a basket.

"I will be back this afternoon and get you a good warm supper," she said.

The Peddler

After Mother had gone, Lem cleaned the floor. He gave the cow and Pig-a-wee their breakfast. Then he and the yellow pup went for a walk in the pine woods.

The day was one of the golden ones when the sun is warm and beautiful. It took Lem a long time to get enough pine wood for the wood basket behind the cabin door.

Then Lem remembered it must be time to see about the fire. As they came near the house, the yellow pup gave a bark and Lem looked up.

There on the cellar step sat a man with a big bundle beside him. The yellow pup ran up to him and barked and barked.

"I am a peddler," the man said to Lem. "Your door was open and I looked in; but there was no one at home, so I just sat down to rest a minute."

"Mother is away," said Lem, and he sat down beside the peddler and looked at the big fat bundle. He wondered how a man no bigger than the peddler could carry so big a bundle.

Then all at once Lem remembered the fire. When he went in to see about it, he asked the peddler to come in, too. The peddler was very much pleased to be asked and went right in.

"Would you like to bring your bundle in?" asked Lem. He wished so much that he could see what the peddler had inside the bundle. Maybe the peddler knew what Lem was thinking about, because he looked at him in a friendly way.

"If you will get me some water," he said, "I will let you see all my things."

How fast Lem got the water for the peddler! Then the peddler opened his bundle.

How many things there were in it—just about everything Lem could think of. But the thing that took his eye was a shiny new bowl. It was bigger than the one that had been broken that morning. It was so shiny that it hurt his eyes to look at it.

How he wished that Mother could see this bowl! Maybe she would buy it from the peddler. She had to have a new bowl to make bread in.

Then Lem wished that he could buy it himself and surprise Mother when she came home. But, oh! He had no money at all—not even a penny.

"Would you like to buy something from me?" the peddler asked.

"Oh yes! Oh yes!" Lem cried. "I would like to buy the beautiful bowl."

Then he told the peddler what had happened to the brown bowl that morning.

"You can buy this bowl for only twenty-five cents," said the peddler.

"It is a beautiful bowl," said Lem, "but I do not have twenty-five cents. It is a long time since I have had even a penny."

The peddler said nothing for a minute. Then he looked at the bowl and he looked at Lem as if he thought of something.

"It must be almost twelve o'clock," he said. "Anyway, I feel hungry. If you will give me some dinner today, I will let you have the bowl."

"Oh, yes!" Lem cried at once, and then, of course, he remembered. There was not any dinner in the house but blueberry pie—Lem's own blueberry pie.

He looked at the lovely brown pie in the middle of the table. He looked again at the beautiful new shiny bowl. Then he turned to the peddler.

"Would a nice, big blueberry pie be all you could eat for dinner?" he asked.

"Show me the pie," said the peddler with a smile. "Then I can tell you."

Lem ran to the table and got the pie.

"How good that looks!" said the peddler. "I can hardly wait to eat it. Yes, I will take the pie, and you take the bowl."

Then the peddler ate a big piece, and how he did enjoy it!

"I never ate such pie in all my days," he said, as he took another piece.

"Yes, blueberry pie is very good," Lem said. "Once I ate two pieces myself."

The peddler looked at Lem and smiled.

"I should like this pie better," he said, "if you would have a piece with me. I do not like to eat all by myself."

"Oh, no," said Lem, "that would not be right."

"Oh, yes, it would," said the peddler. "It is all right if I want you to."

Lem could think of nothing more to say, so he took a piece of pie and gave some to the yellow pup, who looked hungry enough to eat the pie and the pan, too.

Maybe the peddler was not so hungry as he thought he was at first, because he gave Lem another piece, and soon the pie was gone.

Then he gave Lem the shiny bowl, picked up his bundle, and went on up the mountain.

Lem took the bowl and put it on the table. How beautiful it was and oh, if Mother could only see it now!

That afternoon when Mother came home, she saw the bowl on the table.

"Lem," she cried. "Come here and tell me what I see. I can not believe my eyes."

"It is for you—for you, Mother," he cried. "I bought it from a peddler."

"It is a beautiful bowl," said Mother. "But I can not understand, Lem. I thought you didn't have even a penny."

"I didn't have," said Lem. "I bought it with the blueberry pie." He told Mother all about it. How pleased she was!

"Now I think you should have something good for your supper, Lem," said Mother. "Let me think. What can I make for you?"

Lem didn't have to think about that.

"Blueberry pie, another blueberry pie," cried Lem. "That is all I want."

FIDDLE MUSIC

Home to the Mountains

A summer morning in the mountains!

From the deep pine woods on one side of the mountain trail, white smoke floats up and over the treetops. It is not hard to tell that the smoke comes from the chimney of a little mountain cabin.

Would you like to know who lives in this cabin? Everyone from the top of the mountain to Sleepy Hollow Village at its foot, knows. But you do not know, and if you should guess for a year and a day, I would still have to tell you. It is Mr. Carl—the same Mr. Carl who likes birds and lives next door to Alice and Jerry.

Many years ago when Mr. Carl was a boy, he lived in the mountains.

He always remembered the good times he had there. What fun it was to follow the trails, to hide in the deep pine woods, and to look for berries that grew in the open places!

Now every year when summertime comes around again, Mr. Carl comes back to the mountains.

And every year the mountain boys and girls are waiting for him because, you see, they like Mr. Carl just as well as Alice and Jerry do.

Nice things always happen when Mr. Carl is around. So you may be sure that nice things are going to happen in the mountains this summer.

Mountain Tunes

In the early morning when breakfast was over, Mr. Carl liked to put one more pine log into the open fireplace. Then he liked to sit and play the old mountain tunes on his fiddle.

At home Mr. Carl forgot all about that fiddle. But he never forgot to bring it to the mountains.

"There is music in the mountain air," he said, "music in the air."

And there was music when Mr. Carl played his fiddle.

All the boys and girls who lived in the cabins not far away came up the trail to hear the music.

The tunes they liked best were "The Lonesome Trail" and "The Old Pine Tree."

They all stayed for a time to sing the tunes. Then, one by one or two by two, they were off down the trail again.

Sometimes Lem came, too, from his home on the other side of the mountain. But Lem always stayed until Mr. Carl had played every tune he knew. Lem always asked for one tune over again and, of course, Mr. Carl always played it.

The tune Lem always asked for was,
  Charlie went over the mountain,
  To see what he could see;
  But the other side of the mountain,
  Was all there was to see.

It was a jolly tune—so jolly that it made you feel like dancing and dancing.

Anyway, it made Lem feel that way. And sometimes when Mr. Carl was sure no one was around, he danced, too.

"That is the best mountain tune there is, Lem," said Mr. Carl one morning. "Why not learn to play it?"

"Play it!" said Lem. "How can I? What would I play on anyway?"

"I will let you play on my fiddle," said Mr. Carl.

The Voice at the Door

Every morning after that when the other boys and girls had gone, Mr. Carl showed Lem how to play that tune.

It took Lem a long, long time to learn, but at last he could play it—not so well as Mr. Carl, but very well for his first tune. And how he did enjoy it!

One morning Lem was playing the fiddle better than he had ever played before.

I guess it must have been the music that all at once made Mr. Carl stand up and start dancing around the cabin floor. Lem went right on playing.

"Keep it up! Keep it up!" called a voice from the door. "That is fine music!"

It was the peddler! Lem thought of the shiny new bowl and the blueberry pie.

Mr. Carl stopped still. He looked very foolish. But he didn't have to look foolish because in another minute the peddler was right out in the middle of the floor, dancing, too.

"Well! Well!" said the peddler when the music was over at last. "We will soon have another fiddler in the mountains. Who would have thought it? Keep it up, boy! Keep it up!"

Wishing for a Fiddle

All the rest of the summer Lem did keep it up. He learned one tune after another, but the tune he liked best was "Charlie Over the Mountain." He was always happy when he was playing Mr. Carl's fiddle.

Still there were times when Lem was not happy. "How can I be a mountain fiddler?" he wondered. "I won't even have a fiddle when Mr. Carl goes home."

Poor Lem! How he longed for a fiddle of his own. He talked about it to everyone he knew, but no one could help him.

"Where would I get money for a fiddle?" said Father. "I am not rich enough to buy fiddles."

"We must keep our money to buy shoes for winter," said Mother.

"You do not want a fiddle," said Granny May. "Where is the tune box with the morning-glory horn — the one Pig-a-wee got for you with her four little piglets?"

"If it were a melon you wanted," said Preacher Day, "I would give you one from my melon patch. But I can not do anything about a fiddle."

No one could do anything about it. No one could help Lem get a fiddle.

The Fiddling Bee

One golden day just before suppertime, the peddler again made his way up the mountain trail to Mr. Carl's cabin.

"What has become of that boy who played the fiddle?" he asked. "I came all the way up the mountain to find him.

"There will be a fiddling bee tomorrow night in the village. All the old mountain fiddlers from miles around will be there. They like to come and they like to play, but every year they are getting older. Soon there won't be a fiddler left.

"I want them to hear that boy. I will never forget that tune he played and the way we danced."

There never were eyes so big and round and shiny as Lem's were when he heard about the fiddling bee.

The next afternoon Lem and Mr. Carl went down the mountain trail.

It was sundown when they got to the village of Sleepy Hollow. Right in an open place in the middle of the village was a big crowd of people.

When everyone was there, the old mountain fiddlers took their places in front of the crowd and, one by one, they played and played.

Lem thought it was wonderful. The old fiddler who got the prize played some of the tunes that Lem knew best, "The Old Pine Tree" and "The Lonesome Trail."

When the last tune was over, the peddler stepped out from the crowd. He had Mr. Carl's fiddle under his arm.

"My friends!" called the peddler. "There is a new fiddler in the mountains—a fiddler you have never heard before. Come, Lem, and play for us."

Before Lem knew what had happened, he had Mr. Carl's fiddle in his hands.

"Now play 'Charlie Over the Mountain,'" said Mr. Carl.

Lem played as he had never played before.

I guess it must have been the music. Before the tune was ended everyone was dancing and singing.

"You will be the best fiddler in the mountains someday," said one old fiddler after another.

Then the old fiddler who got the prize took Lem's cap around to everyone in the crowd. When the cap came back, it was almost full of pennies.

How Lem hugged the cap that night as he walked proudly up the mountain trail.

"I wish I had pennies enough for a fiddle," he said again and again.

Time to Go

Summer was almost at an end. One day after his dinner of bacon and corn bread, Mr. Carl put out the fire, took his fiddle, and started up the mountain trail.

"It will not hurt me any to give my fiddle to Lem," he said. "I hardly ever play when I am at home. It will be my fault if he is not a mountain fiddler."

When he came to the mountaintop, he looked down on the other side. There was Lem's cabin. As he came nearer, he saw skinny Pig-a-wee, all by herself, rooting in the potato patch near the fence. The yellow pup was playing with a rope.

You could tell by the noise of pots and pans and by the good smell in the air that Lem's mother was working in the kitchen. Maybe she was making another blueberry pie with a hole in the middle for the juice to come through.

Lem was looking for berries at the edge of the woods.

When the yellow pup saw Mr. Carl, he gave a bark and Lem turned around.

"Here you are, Lem," said Mr. Carl. "I have come myself to give you my fiddle."

Only Lem's big brown eyes showed how happy he was. He could not say a word.

"Now," said Mr. Carl, "you must get to be the best fiddler in the mountains."

And do you know? That is just what happened.

COWBOYS and INDIANS

The Great Plains

Do you know what the Great Plains really are? If you live on the plains, of course you know. But if you have never seen the plains, suppose you look at this picture.

Mile after mile of rolling country and grass, grass, grass! Only here and there a house, only here and there a tree, only here and there a river!

The Cattle Country! That is what many people call the plains, for everywhere you look, cattle are grazing. Cowboys on fast horses are riding over the plains to take care of the cattle.

Everywhere you look, rolling country and grass, grass, grass! Cattle grazing, cowboys riding! This is summer on the Great Plains.

Cowboy Jack

Good News

Many miles from Friendly Village was the farm where Jack lived.

It was a morning in early summer, and everything on the farm was still. Not a leaf was moving on the trees near the big white farmhouse.

The hens and ducks were walking about in the barnyard. The cows were eating grass in the pasture not far away.

A summer morning and all was still!

Bang! The door of the farmhouse flew open, and Jack ran down the front steps.

He was so happy that he could not stand still. His blue eyes were shining. His hair was standing up all over his head. On his face was the biggest smile you have ever seen.

Right now he was on his way down the road to the next farmhouse.

Mr. and Mrs. Woods lived there, and Jack had something to tell them. He had to tell someone, you see. The news was too good to keep.

Bang! The door of that farmhouse flew open, and Jack was in the kitchen.

He did not stop to see who was there. He just shouted, "What do you think? Guess where I am going?"

But before anyone could guess, Jack went right on. "I am going out West with Father. I am going to see cowboys. I am going to see Uncle Bill and I have never seen him before."

"Well! Well!" said Mr. Woods, as he got up from the table. "Wait a minute! Sit down and tell me about it. This sounds exciting."

"But I can't wait," said Jack. "I am going in a few minutes. I have just come to say good-by."

"What was that you said?" asked Mrs. Woods, as she came into the kitchen with a pan of berries in her hand. "Going out West? How can we get along without you?"

"I will be back," said Jack. "I am just going for the summer. Good-by."

Mr. and Mrs. Woods stood at the door to watch Jack as he ran down the road.

"Have a good time," they called. "Don't forget to come back."

"I won't," said Jack, and he ran faster than ever. How could he help running? How could anyone help running who was going out West to see cowboys?

The Train Ride

For the next two days Jack and his Father rode on the long train that was going out West.

They ate on the train. They slept on the train. But the thing Jack liked best was to look out of the window.

Things seemed to fly by—farms with big white houses like Jack's house at home—villages that made Jack think of Friendly Village — one big city after another with smoke coming from many chimneys.

Then at last they came to the Great Plains.

How far Jack could see! Most of the time all he could see was grass, grass, grass. Not a house! Not a barn! Not a tree! Just mile after mile of rolling country!

"These are the plains," said Father, "and not far away on a big farm called a ranch, Uncle Bill is waiting for us."

Jack could hardly wait to get there. When the train stopped, he was the first one to jump off.

The Ranch at Last

There, right at the train steps, was a big, jolly-looking man. He looked down at Jack in such a friendly way that Jack knew at once it must be Uncle Bill.

"Well I declare! What a big fellow you are, Jack. It is about time you came out West to see me!"

Jack knew away down inside himself that he liked Uncle Bill and Uncle Bill liked him.

Then Uncle Bill began to talk to Father, and Jack had time to look around.

"Is this a town? Well, I never saw a town like this before," thought Jack. "Just a few houses and only one store. I would not call this a town."

There was only one street in that town. The houses were on one side of the street and the store was on the other.

Jack was just going to run over and look in the store window when he heard Uncle Bill say,

"I declare, Jack! This will never do. You are in a cow country now, and we must make a cowboy out of you in some way or other. Come along with me."

In a minute or two they were all in the store. A big, red-faced, friendly-looking man came up to them.

"What can be done to make a cowboy out of this fellow?" asked Uncle Bill.

"What a foolish question!" said the man. "Give him a cowboy suit and everything that goes with it."

I suppose you can guess what happened then.

When Jack came out of the store, he was no longer Jack. He was Cowboy Jack, all ready for the next exciting thing to happen.

It was a long, hot ride in Uncle Bill's car out to the ranch. Far off to the west, Jack could see mountains. White clouds floated by in the sky overhead. Near at hand he could see cattle grazing. And all around him was rolling country and grass, grass, grass.

Cowboys

It was just about sundown when the car stopped at a long, low ranch house and Jack jumped out.

He was just going into the ranch house with Uncle Bill when he heard the sound of horses' feet.

In a minute he was around the corner of the ranch house, just in time to see five cowboys on horses come riding up. They rode their horses right into a fenced-in place called a corral.

By the time Jack was at the corral, four of the cowboys were off their horses.

The last cowboy, named Red, was having a hard time. Just as he rode into the corral, his horse began to jump. Red did not care. He rode the horse round and round the corral. When the horse was all tired out, he stopped jumping and Red slid off, right by the fence near Jack.

"What a wild horse!" shouted Jack.

"That is the way I like them," said Red. "Hello, fellow! Where did you come from anyway? You look like a real cowboy."

"I'm not a real cowboy now, but soon I'm going to be," called Jack.

The rest of the cowboys were just coming up to talk to Jack, when a voice called, "Come and get it!"

All the cowboys started to run and Jack ran, too. He didn't know what they were going to get, but whatever it was, he was going to get it, too.

They ran right to a long, low house not far from the corral.

Of course, the cowboys got there first, but Jack was right behind them.

As soon as Jack was in the door, he knew what he was going to get.

There was a smell of good things in the air. The cook had supper all ready on the table waiting for them. Jack did not wait to be asked. He just sat down with the cowboys and ate and ate.

When supper was over, all the cowboys and Jack sat on the steps of the cook-house.

One of the cowboys, named Charlie, took out his mouth organ, and how he did play!

Before many minutes all the cowboys were singing one cowboy song after another.

There was one song Jack could sing, too. That was "Home on the Range." He never knew what a good song that was until he heard the cowboys sing.

Then out from the cook-house came the cook with his fiddle in his hand. Charlie played the mouth organ, the cook fiddled, and the songs started all over again.

"What do you call this anyway? A singing bee or a fiddling bee and who gets the prize?" called a voice. There stood Uncle Bill. Father was with him.

"Really I think it is time for big cowboys and little cowboys to be in bed," said Father.

When Jack heard the word "bed," he thought of something. Right next to the cook-house was another low house with beds all around the sides. Oh, how he wished that he could sleep there with the cowboys!

Red must have guessed what Jack was thinking, for all at once he stood up.

"Come on, Cowboy!" he said to Jack. "There is a bed right next to mine and that is where you belong."

Jack looked at Father and Uncle Bill and waited a minute. But they did not say "No." So he went with Red.

"Come and get it!"

Jack was sure he had not been asleep a minute when he heard that call.

Every cowboy was out of bed and dressed before Jack was through thinking how sleepy he was.

"Out with you!" called Red, as he threw some cold water into Jack's sleepy eyes. "Come and get it, Cowboy!"

Jack was out in a hurry after that. What a big breakfast he had and what a big breakfast all the cowboys had!

The sun was just coming up as Jack stood by the corral and watched the cowboys ride away.

The Cow Pony

Then Jack walked up to the ranch house to find Father and Uncle Bill. Uncle Bill was just coming out of the door.

"Well, I declare!" said Uncle Bill, smiling down at Jack. "A cowboy on foot! A cowboy on foot is no cowboy at all! Seems to me there is a cow pony down in the pasture waiting for you."

And sure enough, down in the pasture waiting for Jack was a cow pony.

"This pony knows the range, Jack. The range is the name we give to the great plains where the cattle graze. Someday when you learn to ride this pony well, you can go out on the range with Red."

How glad Jack was that he had learned to ride a little on the farm back home. All morning he rode the cow pony.

When afternoon came, he was so tired that he had a long sleep.

At sundown when the cowboys rode into the corral again, Jack on his cow pony was waiting for them.

"Just as soon as I can ride well enough, I'm going out on the range with you, Red," he called.

"What do you know about that!" said Red. "Come on! I'll show you how to ride."

Then Red showed Jack the right way to get on his pony. Jack did just as Red told him to do and soon he learned the right way.

Every night after that Jack learned a little more—but only a little, because the minute Red heard the call, "Come and get it," he forgot all about horses and started for the cook-house. When a cowboy is hungry, he is very hungry, and there is only one thing to be done about it. That is one way in which cowboys and all boys are just alike.

A Day on the Range

As the days went by, Jack learned to ride the cow pony better and better.

At last the day came when Red said, "Tomorrow I will be alone on the range, Jack. How about coming with me?"

Red did not have to ask a second time.

Before sun-up the next morning Red called to Jack, "Hop out, Cowboy."

All morning long Jack rode with Red over the range. He never knew until that day how big the Great Plains really were.

Here and there they came upon cattle and horses grazing. Red rode near enough to them to see that all was well. Then on he and Jack would ride again.

Once they even came upon some wild horses grazing near a water hole. The wild horses were up and away as soon as they saw the cowboys.

"Someday I'm going to catch one with my rope," said Red.

How Jack did wish he could be around when that happened!

About twelve o'clock they stopped near a water hole to cook their dinner.

Red looked around for a safe place to make a fire. He was very careful to see that the grass didn't catch fire.

Then they cooked their dinner right over the open fire—flapjacks and bacon. Have you ever had a dinner like that? Jack never had—and how he did enjoy it!

Then as Red and Jack rested under a tree near the water hole, the best thing of all happened.

Red showed Jack how to throw the long rope that cowboys always carry with them. He twirled the long rope round and round and then threw it right over the head of one of the cows that was grazing near by. He threw the rope again and again but he never missed.

Then of course Jack had to try, too. But the rope was too big for Jack, and he missed every time.

"Here is a small rope," said Red at last. "Try your hand at this, Jack."

And then after about twenty-five times, Jack did throw the small rope right over his cow pony's head. I am sure that pony was just as surprised as Jack was when that happened. Anyway, he started to run away, and Red had to help Jack hold him.

All that long, hot afternoon, Jack and Red rode the range.

Just as they started for home, Red heard something. He knew at once what it was.

"A cow in trouble, Jack! Come on!" he said, and away he rode. Jack followed.

When Jack rode up to Red, Red had stopped at the edge of a big hole. Down in the hole was a cow that could not get out.

Red threw his rope right over the cow's horns. Then he tied the rope to the front of his saddle. The horse pulled and helped the cow out of the hole.

"Our ropes are good for many things, Jack," said Red, "and this is one of them. Come on! We must hurry home!"

It was a happy but tired Jack who rode into the corral that night—too tired to eat much—too tired to sing "Home on the Range"—too tired to tell Father and Uncle Bill all that had happened—too tired to do anything but sleep.

The next morning Jack's tired feeling was all forgotten, and he was ready to begin all over again.

This was the beginning of many happy days on the range. The more Jack rode, the more he liked it.

When summer was over and it was time to go home again, no one was surprised to hear him say,

"I'll be right back again next summer, and when I grow up, I'm going to be a cowboy. That is what I'm going to be."

Singing Boy

A Good Year

Not many miles to the west of Uncle Bill's ranch lived some Navaho Indians —a father, a mother, and a little Indian boy and girl.

The father was called "Snapping Turtle"; the mother, "Dark Eyes." Their happy little Indian girl was called "Silver Cloud." The boy, who could ride his pony better than any Indian boy for miles around, was called "Singing Boy."

No other Indians were as happy as they.

All through the long summer days, Snapping Turtle was at work making rings and other beautiful things of silver.

Dark Eyes was seated not far away in the doorway of the Indian house. She was making the beautiful Navaho blankets.

Snapping Turtle and Dark Eyes were happy as they worked, and they sang the lovely old songs of the Navaho people.

Most of the time Singing Boy was out with the cattle, looking here and there for the best grazing places.

Silver Cloud's work was to take care of the sheep. Every morning as she opened the gate of the corral to let out the sheep, White-foot, the long-haired sheep dog, was at her side.

White-foot had been Silver Cloud's and Singing Boy's friend, helper, and play-fellow for seven long years.

Now summer was almost over.

The white people who had come to the Indian country had bought many of Snapping Turtle's silver rings and many of Dark Eyes' beautiful blankets. The Indian bowl in its hiding place in the corner of the hogan, or Indian house, was almost full of money.

Singing Boy and Silver Cloud had been so careful to find the best grazing places that the cattle and sheep had grown very fat.

All these were good things, and because of them the family of Snapping Turtle was very happy.

The Feast of Thanksgiving

One day Snapping Turtle said to his wife, "After two more sleeps in the hogan we will go to the foot of Big Mountain. There we will join all the rest of the Navaho people in the feast of Thanksgiving for the good things that have come to us. We will stay for three days and nights. Come, let us make ready!"

When Singing Boy and Silver Cloud heard Snapping Turtle, they ran to the spring and back again because they were so delighted. There would be feasting and dancing at Big Mountain, and they longed to go.

The day before the last sleep, Snapping Turtle took the cattle to the grazing ground near the river. Singing Boy with the help of Silver Cloud took food and water to the sheep in the corral—enough to last for three days and three nights.

When the morning of the feast day
came, everyone in the hogan was up
before the sun.

Singing Boy remembered that the last
thing he must do was to leave bread and
water for White-foot, his friend and play-
fellow. He picked up the water basket
and ran along the trail to the spring.

He had just filled the basket when high
overhead he heard the sound of an airplane. He ran shouting to the hogan so
that Silver Cloud could see it, too. The
water basket for White-foot was forgotten.

The sun had come up over Big Mountain
before the little family was on its way to
the feast.

Snapping Turtle drove the wagon, and Dark Eyes and Silver Cloud sat beside him on the seat.

Because Singing Boy could ride so well, he followed the wagon on Sure-foot, his own little pony.

"It has been a good year," said Snapping Turtle, as they drove along. "We must dance well and sing many songs to show our thanks."

All through the long, hot morning they followed the trail. When at last they came to Big Mountain, they could see on every side the happy faces of friends and hear the sound of singing voices.

That afternoon Snapping Turtle and his family made camp under some trees which were not far from the feast fires.

The races were just beginning. Singing
Boy was told that the best race of all was
to come at sun-up the next morning—a
pony race for all the Indian boys. The
boy who could win that race would get a
silver dollar.

Oh, how Singing Boy wanted to win
that race! How he wanted to have a
dollar of his own! He could win the race.
He knew he could. On the back of his
own little pony he could ride faster than
any other Indian boy.

Just as the sun was going down, Singing Boy remembered something—remembered so suddenly that he stood still. He could not move!

The basket he had filled with water for White-foot was still at the spring. He had forgotten it when the airplane came flying through the sky.

White-foot was tied fast near the door of the hogan—White-foot, who had been Singing Boy's friend, helper, and play-fellow for seven long years. He could not get water for himself.

Singing Boy knew what he must do.
First of all, tomorrow's race and the prize
he wanted so much must be forgotten.
He must go back to the hogan that very
night and give White-foot some water.

When Snapping Turtle heard the story,
he said, "You are right! It will soon be
night, but all will be well with you. Your
pony will know the way. Go at once!
White-foot is waiting for you."

Singing Boy jumped on the back of
Sure-foot, his pony. He turned for a last
look at the feasting place.

"I can not go," he thought. "I must stay
for the race tomorrow morning. I can win
the silver dollar. I know I can."

Then once more he thought of White-foot
tied fast without water.

"We must not turn back," he said to
his pony. "Fly, little pony! We go to
help White-foot, our friend."

The pony seemed to understand, for he
ran like the wind along the trail.

On and on went Singing Boy and his
pony—on and on until it began to grow
dark and stars came out high overhead.

Night came, but Singing Boy was not
afraid.

Then came the first call of the night
bird, and the Indian boy thought he had
never heard such a lovely song.

On and on went the little pony. Now
they had come to the trees by the water
hole and were almost home.

When they came to the hogan, Singing
Boy jumped from his pony.

"I am coming, White-foot," he called, as he raced to the spring.

He filled the basket with cold water and ran back to where White-foot was tied.

How glad White-foot was to see him! It seemed almost as if he said, "All day I have wanted water. I knew you would come, Singing Boy."

Then Singing Boy got food and water for himself and his pony, and food and more water for White-foot.

"All is well," he said with a low laugh. Then he went to sleep in the hogan.

As the sun came over the mountaintop, he was on his way back to the feasting— too late for the race—too late to win the silver dollar. But Singing Boy was happy.

The
SILVER BRACELET

The Lucky Stone

The Bluebird sings,
Early in the morning
The Bluebird sings,
Beautiful as the sky,
The Bluebird.

But I have a stone,
A sky-blue stone,
Beautiful as the bluebird,
Beautiful as the sky,
My lucky stone.

Singing Boy sat on the ground in the door of the hogan singing softly to himself. He was turning over and over in his hand a small, sky-blue stone called a turquoise. As he sang, he put the stone carefully on the ground before him.

Then from a string about his neck Singing Boy took another sky-blue stone. There was a smile on the dark face of the Indian boy as he placed the two stones side by side.

"My lucky stones," he said, as he looked from one to the other. "Now only good things can happen to Singing Boy."

The turquoise that he took from about his neck had been Singing Boy's lucky stone for many years—ever since he was a baby in the hogan of Snapping Turtle.

Like every other Navaho Indian, he never forgot to carry his lucky stone.

"Luck goes where the turquoise goes." So say the Navahos.

The second turquoise had come to Singing Boy in another way.

Not many days before, Big Smoke and his family, who lived in the hogan by the water hole, had gone to the white man's trading post to sell blankets and to buy food.

Big Smoke's sheep and cattle were left to the care of Singing Boy. Every day he took them to the best grazing places and gave them water.

Now after five days, Big Smoke and his family were at home again.

This morning as Singing Boy rode by the water hole on Sure-foot, his own little pony, Big Smoke was standing in the door of his hogan.

"You have cared well for my sheep and cattle," he called. "Here is something for you from the trading post of the white man." Then he put into Singing Boy's hand the sky-blue turquoise.

This is how the second turquoise had come to Singing Boy. This is why he was sitting in the door of the hogan looking at his lucky stones and singing:

"Beautiful as the bluebird,
Beautiful as the sky,
My lucky stones."

Singing Boy knew that the first stone —the one he had had for many years— must be tied again on the string about his neck. There it must stay to keep trouble away and to bring him good luck.

But the other—the new stone. What should he do with that?

For three moons he had been learning from Snapping Turtle, his father, how to work in silver. Could he make a lovely shining thing to hold his lucky stone?

An ear-ring? Should he make that? No! There must be two ear-rings and he had only one stone. A ring? No! The new turquoise was too small for that.

Singing Boy knew what he would make —a lovely silver bracelet. He could do that. He would begin at once.

On one end of the bracelet he would put the picture of falling rain. On the other end would be the cloud ladder going to the sky. And in the middle, in a place all its own, he would put the sky-blue turquoise.

With a low laugh Singing Boy jumped to his feet. With one lucky stone on his neck and the other in his hand, he ran round the hogan to the workbench of Snapping Turtle.

Tap, tap, tap, went Singing Boy's hammer through the long, hot afternoon. Tap, tap, tap, it went through the next afternoon and the next.

He must not hurry. Snapping Turtle had told him that the piece of silver must be hammered long and well.

Tap, tap, tap, went the hammer until the piece of silver had grown long and smooth—tap, tap, tap, until Snapping Turtle said, "It is well."

Then carefully at one end Singing Boy put the picture of falling rain—carefully at the other end the cloud ladder going to the sky. And in the middle, in a place all its own, he put the lucky stone.

When the bracelet was done, Singing Boy held it high overhead. The sun was shining full upon it. By the glad look in his eyes and the smile on his face, you could tell how happy he was.

"It is mine," he said again and again. "Rain to make things grow for me! A cloud ladder to take me to the sky! A turquoise to bring me good luck! Surely my bracelet is a beautiful thing."

He ran into the hogan to show it to Dark Eyes and Silver Cloud. As he ran, he sang again the Indian song,

> "Beautiful as the sky,
> My lucky stone."

The Trading Post

One morning in late summer, the family of Snapping Turtle was up before the sun. They were going to the trading post of the white man many miles away.

There they would sell the blankets that Dark Eyes had been making, and Snapping Turtle's rings and bracelets.

Snapping Turtle drove the wagon, just as he had done when they had gone to the feast at Big Mountain. Dark Eyes and Silver Cloud sat beside him.

Because Singing Boy could ride so well, he rode ahead on Sure-foot, his own little pony. He seemed to race like the wind along the trail to the trading post. On his arm was the silver bracelet.

This same morning, Jack on the ranch was talking things over with Uncle Bill.

"I want to ask a question," said Jack. "I thought when I came out West, I would see Indians. I have been here almost all summer and I have not seen one Indian. Don't you have any around here?"

"I knew I should take you to the trading post," said Uncle Bill, as he ran his hand through his hair. "But I seem to have forgotten all about it. I'll try to go with you today. We can't let you go home without seeing Indians. Now see how fast you can get ready."

Jack hoped they could go on horseback, but Uncle Bill said, "No!" So Jack let his pony out of the corral to graze in the pasture. Then he hopped into the car.

"Keep your eyes open, Jack," said Uncle
Bill, after they had gone many miles to
the west and were leaving the great rolling plains behind them. "It won't be long
now until you see Indians."

In just a few minutes an Indian boy on
a pony rode right across the road in front
of them. Jack could not believe his eyes
as he watched him ride by.

"Look, Uncle Bill, look!" he cried. "He
can ride without even a saddle!"

"I declare!" said Uncle Bill. "He is a
fine rider for such a little fellow."

When they came to the trading post, Jack saw that it was just a big store.

Near by was the Indian camp ground. When the Indian boys saw Jack, one of them played a mouth organ. Another twirled a rope. Another began to dance.

Inside, the store was filled with Indians. Everyone had blankets to sell. Everyone had rings and bracelets. Everyone seemed to want Uncle Bill and Jack to buy everything, and all at once.

"What funny names these Indians have," thought Jack—"Big Horn, Shining Star, Silver Moon."

Then Jack began to look around to see what he could buy for Mother. A ring— she would like a ring. Here was just the ring he wanted—one silver leaf after another, all joined together.

Jack was just going to take his money out of his pocket, when suddenly an Indian boy on a pony rode up to the door.

"Look, Uncle Bill," Jack called, as the Indian boy slid from his pony. "It is the same boy we saw. I'm sure it is. The one who rode without a saddle."

Of course it was Singing Boy, and in just a minute he took his place with the other Indians, holding in his hand a beautiful silver bracelet.

"Did you make it? How could you?" Jack said, as he ran up to Singing Boy.

When Jack heard about the falling rain, the cloud ladder going to the sky, and the sky-blue lucky stone, he knew at once that the bracelet was just what he wanted for Mother.

"Will you sell it to me? Will you sell it to me for this?" he said, as he took out of his pocket a shiny silver dollar.

Singing Boy's eyes were round with surprise. A real silver dollar—just like the one he had hoped to win in the pony race at Big Mountain. A real silver dollar all his own! This was what his lucky stone had done for him.

As he handed the bracelet to Jack, it was hard to tell who was more pleased— Jack with the bracelet or Singing Boy with his silver dollar.

A few days later, the train door closed with a bang and Jack, dressed in his cowboy suit, was on his way back home.

He ate on the train, he slept on the train, but some of the time he just sat thinking—thinking of the days when he rode the range with Red, of the dinners they had cooked together, and of the good flapjacks and bacon. He wondered if his pony would know him when he came back next year. He thought of the dark-faced Indian boy and the silver bracelet.

And far away to the west in the hogan of Snapping Turtle, the silver dollar was safe in its hiding place. At the workbench behind the hogan, Singing Boy's hammer was going tap, tap, tap. He was making another silver bracelet.

SEASHORE DAYS

Down by the Sea

Do you know what the sea really looks like? If you live by the sea, of course you know. But if you have never seen the sea, suppose you look at this picture.

Water—more water than you have ever seen before—sometimes green, sometimes gray, sometimes blue as turquoise! White-capped waves that come rolling in and splash upon the land! This is the sea.

The land at the edge of the sea is called
the seashore. Sometimes it is covered with
great rocks where the white-capped waves
splash high.

Sometimes it is low and smooth and
covered with white sand. Here boys and
girls like to race and play. Sometimes
they find sea animals and fish and other
wonderful things in the sand.

A Summer by the Sea

The First Day at the Shore

Early one summer morning, a train stopped at a little fishing village by the sea, and Bobby and Billy and Mother got off.

Bobby and Billy had been out West. They had been to the mountains. They had even been to the North Woods. But they had never been to the seashore.

Their eyes were big with surprise as they stood on the sandy shore and saw before them the great blue ocean.

"Come, Billy," called Bobby, and away he ran right down to the edge of the waves.

But Billy just stood still and looked and looked. He never had thought there could be so much water in all the world. The great white-capped waves came rolling in. What a noise each one made as it splashed upon the shore! And all up and down the shore as far as he could see—sand, sand, sand!

Billy forgot his surprise and raced after Bobby. In just a minute their shoes and stockings were off, and the waves were rolling over their feet.

Captain Lee

This was the beginning of many happy days for Bobby and Billy. All summer long they lived in the little fishing village that climbed the hill. All summer they raced and played on the sandy shore.

Soon everyone in the fishing village knew Bobby and Billy. Everyone knew them because they were twins and because they asked so many questions.

The best friend Bobby and Billy had was Captain Lee. He was an old sea captain and he knew all there was to know about the sea.

He lived in the stone house with the red roof that stood on top of the hill.

Captain Lee was too old now to go to sea. But he still wore his captain's suit and his captain's cap. Everyone called him Captain Lee. He liked that much better than being called Mr. All sea captains feel the same way.

Captain Lee liked to sit at his work-bench under the apple tree. Then he could look out to sea as he hammered away, tap, tap, tap.

It was good luck for Bobby and Billy when they found him there, because he always had a story to tell of the days when he sailed the seas.

Mrs. Lee did not like the sea, but she did like the captain and she did like to bake. Most of the time she stayed in the kitchen baking good things for him to eat.

It would be hard to tell you all the interesting things Bobby and Billy learned from Captain Lee that summer.

Every day, at some time or other, they came racing up the hill to find him. Then all three together, they started out to see how many interesting things they could find—shells, fish, and queer sea animals.

Mr. Crab

One afternoon Bobby walked ahead all by himself along the sandy shore.

All at once he looked down. There at his feet was a little hole in the sand. Something was coming out of the hole. If Bobby had not seen it move, he never would have guessed that it was there. It was just the color of the sand. At first he thought it was a spider, but he had never seen a spider as big as that.

In another minute the queer-looking animal was out of the hole and right on the sand in front of him.

The back of the animal was covered with a hard shell, and on each side were four queer-looking legs. In front were two things that looked for all the world like two big pincers.

When Bobby leaned over for a better look, he saw two stalks growing right out of that queer thing's head. On the end of each stalk was an eye. Just as Bobby looked, the stalks and the eyes went right back into its head. Then suddenly, out they came again.

All at once the queer thing started away—not straight ahead, but sideways. How fast it did go! Bobby was sure he had never seen anything move so fast before.

"Hurry! Hurry! Come and see! Come and see!" he shouted.

"What is it? What is it?" shouted Billy, as he raced up the sand.

But by this time the queer thing had made another hole in the smooth sand and was nowhere to be seen.

"That is just an old sand crab," said Captain Lee when Bobby told him about it. "There are many kinds of crabs on this shore—green crabs, blue crabs, spider crabs. Look, here is another."

Billy did not even see the crab. It was so much the color of the sand. But how he jumped when Captain Lee called, "Look out, Billy! That fellow has pincers and he can use them, too."

Then Billy looked hard and he saw another sand crab with the same queer eyes and legs and the same big pincers.

Not long after this a man came walking along the shore with a basket.

"What do you think you have here?" asked the Captain, as the man held up the basket for him to see.

Bobby and Billy looked, too. There were crabs in that basket, but they looked as if they had lost their shells.

"Upon my word! Soft-shelled crabs!" said Captain Lee. "And they are blue crabs at that. I'll have some for my dinner. Go right up the hill to Mrs. Lee with that basket."

"Soft-shelled crabs?" asked Billy. "These crabs haven't any shells at all."

"Oh, yes, they have," said Captain Lee. "They are getting new ones."

Then he told them that crabs outgrow their shells just as boys outgrow their coats. When crabs grow too big for their shells, the shells crack. Then the crabs pull themselves out, legs, pincers and all. Their backs are covered with something sticky. This is the time when men, sea animals, and fish like best to eat them. So they hide away in a safe place until that sticky something becomes hard and makes a new shell.

Captain Lee did not want to stay on the shore much longer after he saw that basket of soft-shelled crabs. I suppose he was thinking how good they were going to taste.

"Now you two might just as well stay for dinner and help me eat the crabs," he said, as they climbed the hill.

Bobby and Billy were sure they wanted to stay for dinner. But they were not sure they wanted to eat crabs.

But you know how it is. Sometimes the things you think are not going to be good at all, are the best things you ever tasted. All I know is that when dinner was over, Bobby and Billy wished there had been many more crabs in that big basket.

 # Questions

Seashore Surprises

One day everyone in the fishing village asked everyone else a question.

Mrs. Plain asked Mrs. White when she saw her on the corner of High Street. Mrs. White asked Mrs. Lee, and Mrs. Lee asked Mrs. Green.

The storekeeper asked that question of everyone who came into his store. The milkman, when he left his milk bottles, always stopped long enough to ask that question of the lady in the kitchen.

The question was always the same. "Are you going to the clambake?" And everyone in the village answered, "Yes."

When I said everyone asked the same question, I forgot Bobby and Billy.

When Captain Lee asked, "Are you going to the clambake?" they said,

"Yes, we are going. But what is it? How do we get there? What are clams? Who is going to bake them? What—"

"That's enough! That's enough!" said Captain Lee, and he put his hands over his ears to keep out the rest of their questions. "If you don't know anything about clams, it is high time you did. We will go and dig some."

Captain Lee went into the house. When he came out, he had a pail and something that looked like a rake. Of course, that started the questions all over again.

"What are they for? What are you going to do with them?"

"Now just keep still for five minutes and come along," said the Captain.

He took them far down the shore to a place where the sand was all full of holes. Something must have made the holes. What was it?

Billy leaned over to see if he could see what was down in one hole. At first he could not see anything. Suddenly some water came right up out of the hole.

Billy jumped. "Oh! Oh!" he shouted. "I wonder what that was!"

"A clam," laughed the Captain, and he began to dig down into the sand with his rake. In less than a minute up came a shell—two shells fastened together.

"It is alive! It is alive!" shouted Billy.

And sure enough, just at that minute the two shells opened. Out came a long neck. Then back the neck went and the two shells closed again.

"Yes, Mr. Clam is alive inside his house, all ready to be baked for your dinner tomorrow," said the Captain.

For some time after this, Captain Lee went right on digging clams.

It surely pays to know how to do things well. In no time at all, Captain Lee had that pail full of clams. He knew just where to find them and he never cracked the shells.

As for Bobby and Billy—they cracked almost every shell they came to, and a clam with its shell cracked is no good at all.

When the pail was full, they went back up the hill and left it on the gatepost for Mrs. Lee. She washed each clam to get out the sand. Then she put all the clams into a big pail of water.

The Clambake on the Shore

You know I told you that Bobby and Billy raced up the hill every day to find the Captain. But the next morning it was the other way around. The Captain rode down the hill to find them.

"Come on!" he called. "No time to be lazy on the morning of a clambake!"

Bobby and Billy came racing out of the house, and there were the Captain and another man on the front seat of a wagon full of wood.

"Now don't begin asking questions," said the Captain. "This wood is for the fire to bake the clams. Hop up here in a hurry."

Bobby and Billy did their best to keep still, but at last Bobby could stand it no longer. He turned to Captain Lee and said softly, "Why do you have to have so much wood? Are you going to bake all the clams on the shore?"

"No, not all," laughed the Captain. "But we are going to bake these." And he pulled out from under the seat the pail of clams they had helped him dig. "I'm not trading these clams for all the rest of the clams on the seashore."

Soon they came to a place on the shore where there were many flat rocks. Here the man stopped the wagon and they all helped to carry out the wood.

It pays to know how to do things well. The man knew just how to make the fire. He put some pieces of wood one way and some another. Right among the pieces of wood he put the rocks, each rock in its right place. Then he started the fire and what a fire it was! The biggest fire Bobby and Billy had ever, ever, ever seen!

"It takes a big fire to bake clams for everyone in a fishing village," said the man, and he put on more and more wood.

When at last the fire was just right and the rocks were very, very hot, he covered every rock with seaweed.

Now came the most interesting time of all.

Right on top of the wet seaweed Captain Lee and the man put potatoes. Bobby and Billy were sure there were ten potatoes for everyone in the fishing village. And then corn—ears and ears and ears of corn! And after that clams—clams and clams and more clams!

Then, last of all, the man covered the potatoes, the corn, and the clams with more wet seaweed—seaweed that grew hot from the rocks and steamed and steamed and steamed.

How much food there was and oh, how good it smelled!

Then, a few at a time, the people began to come from the fishing village.

What a shore dinner that was! Everyone sat on blankets on the sand and ate and ate and ate.

When dinner was over, all the boys and girls ran races. When they were too tired for that, they looked for shells along the shore.

Bobby and Billy found some little shells. Mother showed them how to make a hole in each one. Then they put them on a string and made a bracelet out of them.

Everyone stayed on the shore until the moon came up over the ocean. Then Bobby and Billy and Mother started for home.

You may know that Bobby and Billy were tired, for all the way home they never asked one question—no, not one.

THE JOKE ON MRS. LEE

Big Words

Do you like to use big words—words just like the ones grown-up people use? Sometimes you don't know just what the words mean, but they sound well and you like to say them over and over.

The word Bobby and Billy liked to say was "discovery." One day they heard Mother telling Mrs. Gray about someone who had made an interesting discovery. Of course they wanted to know what that was. It sounded so big and exciting.

"Oh," said Mother, "when someone finds something that he never expected to find —well, that is a discovery."

All that day Bobby and Billy said over and over again, "Discovery, discovery."

That night when Bobby and Billy were all covered up in bed, Bobby said, "Why can't we make some kind of discovery?"

"We can," said Billy. "We will look and look until we find something we never expected to find. Then that will be a discovery."

So the next morning they started out.

First they walked along the seashore. They had no time to take off their shoes and stockings and play in the waves. They had no time to look at the queer old sand crabs with their big pincers — crabs that looked like big spiders to Bobby. No time to dig for clams with the rake Captain Lee gave them! No time to pull the wet seaweed and look for shells!

They were going to make a discovery.

Bobby and Billy walked along by the ocean until they came to the flat rocks that had been used for the clambake. Here they found a sticky, soft-shelled crab down among the rocks. But that was not a real discovery. They had seen soft-shelled crabs before.

So back they came. Then they went straight up the hill to the house with the red roof where Captain Lee lived.

The Captain was under the apple tree. Mrs. Lee came out of the house with a pail in her hand, and the two of them began to talk as fast as ever they could.

Someone Is Coming

"He will be here for dinner. What are we going to have?" said Captain Lee.

"I'll give him chicken baked just as he likes it," said Mrs. Lee, "and the apple pie he talks so much about. I suppose I'll have to have steamed clams or else he won't think it is a dinner."

"Well, there is nothing too good for him," answered the Captain.

"I wonder what he will bring me this time," said Mrs. Lee. "He never forgets to bring me something interesting."

Just at that minute the Captain looked up, and there stood Bobby and Billy.

"Where in the world did you come from? Do you know who has just come to town? My old ship the 'Betsy Lee' is home from South America, and the new captain will be here for dinner."

What exciting news for Bobby and Billy! A real sea captain coming for dinner. They sat under the apple tree with Mrs. Lee and the Captain and talked and talked.

Time went on. Mrs. Lee went into the house to look after the dinner. This was not an everyday dinner, you see.

Bobby and Billy knew they should go home. It was dinner time for them, too. But how could they go when a real sea captain would soon be here?

Captain Sandy

Then up the street came Captain Sandy. He wore a white suit, and a captain's cap just like Captain Lee's. He had red whiskers and his hair was the same color. He looked very jolly and in his hand he had a big cage.

"Hello, hello!" shouted Captain Lee.

"By my sea whiskers, I'm glad to see you," called Captain Sandy.

"What in the world have you there?" said Captain Lee when he saw the cage.

"There is something alive in it! It is a monkey!" shouted Bobby and Billy.

"What do you think of him?" asked Captain Sandy. "He sailed all the way from South America with me."

"What are you going to do with him now?" asked Captain Lee.

"Give him to Mrs. Lee," answered Captain Sandy. "Give him to Mrs. Lee."

Bobby and Billy and Captain Lee just shouted. A monkey from South America for Mrs. Lee. What would she say about that?

Their shouts brought Mrs. Lee to the door.

"I have a friend from South America with me," called Captain Sandy when he saw her. "Have you dinner for two?"

"My land—a monkey! Will you never stop playing jokes?" asked Mrs. Lee.

"Oh, come now, come!" said Captain Sandy. "This is no joke. He is a fine monkey. I brought him all the way from South America just for you." Then he laughed until he shook all over.

"I wish you had lost him on the way," said Mrs. Lee. "I haven't any place for a monkey. If you brought him for me, you can just take him back. Come in now, and stop your joking. I have the best chicken dinner you ever tasted."

The two captains went into the house. The monkey sat in his cage on the step.

Then Bobby and Billy ran home to their dinner. Of course they told Mother about Captain Sandy and the monkey.

"We never expected to see a real sea captain with a monkey," said Billy. "We made a discovery—a real discovery."

When they went out to play again, Mother said, "Now don't go to Captain Lee's house any more today. You will just be in the way."

"Maybe we could look through the fence and see the monkey," said Bobby.

"Yes," said Mother, "but don't go in."

So Bobby and Billy stood right at the place where the sunflower stalks grew high over the fence, and no one inside could see them. Then each one looked through the cracks in the fence.

The monkey was still on the step.

At last the side door opened. Mrs. Lee and the captains came out and sat under the apple tree and laughed and talked.

Then, when the afternoon was almost over, Captain Sandy got up in a hurry.

"By my sea whiskers, I must be going," he said. "I am to be back on the ship by six o'clock. I had such a good dinner that I am too lazy to move."

"Don't forget to come again," said Captain Lee.

"And don't forget to take your friend with you," said Mrs. Lee.

"Now, now," said Captain Sandy, "surely you don't mean that, do you?"

"I mean every word of it," said Mrs. Lee. "What would I do with a monkey?"

Captain Sandy's Joke

The end of it was that Captain Sandy said good-by and walked down the street with that cage in his hand. Of course you know who walked with him.

Bobby and Billy looked at the monkey in the cage, and they wished — oh, how they wished — that Mrs. Lee had wanted to keep him.

"Maybe she will still get this monkey," said Captain Sandy, and his eyes were dancing with fun.

After they had walked along the shore for a time, Captain Sandy turned around and started up the hill again. Bobby and Billy were too surprised to ask a question.

Right back to Captain Lee's house he went. He stood by the gate and listened.

"I thought so," he said softly. "The dishes had to be washed. The two of them are at it. Now is my time."

Then what do you think he did? He walked right into that garden and fastened the cage to the apple tree.

"Don't you tell," he said to Bobby and Billy, as he walked away. "Don't you tell."

Before long Captain and Mrs. Lee came out of the door together.

"Really, my dear, I'm proud of you," said the Captain. "You played a good joke on Captain Sandy that time."

"Yes, I did," said Mrs. Lee with a smile. "He thought bringing me a monkey was a big joke. But it never pays to play a joke on me."

"You are right," answered the Captain. "But—look, my dear, look!"

And there, in the cage fastened to the apple tree, Mrs. Lee saw the monkey.

"Well of all things," said Mrs. Lee. "That is just like Captain Sandy. The minute your back is turned, he plays another joke. I'll send this monkey right back to him."

"Don't be in such a hurry," said the Captain. "It is too late to send that monkey back today. Wait until tomorrow. Anyway, it is not the monkey's fault. Look at him! How hungry and lonesome he looks!"

Now Mrs. Lee could not stand to see any animal hungry—not even a monkey. She went right into the house and came out with a big banana in her hand.

By this time Bobby and Billy were over the fence. "Captain Sandy is gone, so it is all right to go in now," said Bobby.

"Do you know how this monkey got back here?" asked Mrs. Lee, as she gave the banana to the monkey. "Someone around here has been up to mischief."

But Bobby and Billy did not say a word.

Mrs. Lee's Joke

"You know more than you are telling," said Mrs. Lee with a smile.

The monkey gobbled up the banana, and Mrs. Lee liked him a little better. Then she gave him another banana, and she liked him even more.

When she saw how interested and delighted Bobby and Billy were and how much they wanted to play with the monkey, she knew she could not send him away. She just could not do that.

"Well," she said, as she opened the door of the cage, "I'll keep you after all, Little Monkey. I'll keep you after all and call you Sandy. That will be the best joke of all."

DID YOU EVER

Away Down South

Once upon a time away down South where the sun shines most of the time, there was a pretty green house with a rosebush growing over the door.

There was a white fence, too, where flowers of all colors looked through the cracks to see what was going on outside.

In front of the house was a chinaberry
tree that looked like a big umbrella.

Other trees grew all around the house
and looked over the high back fence into
the woods.

It was a lovely place to live in, this
pretty green house with the rosebush
growing over the door.

Did You Ever

The House on Wheels

Early in the month of June, Paddy left his home in Friendly Village and went away down South to stay all summer with Grandmother and Grandfather.

All summer long he lived in the pretty green house with the rosebush growing over the door.

It was great fun to climb the chinaberry tree that looked like a big umbrella. Paddy had a seat up there. He liked to watch what was coming down the long white road.

One day just about sundown, Paddy
was having a fine time, seated high up
in the umbrella tree. All at once he saw
something he had never expected to see.

"Oh! Oh! See what I see!" he cried.
"Did you ever? It is a house on wheels.
There is a horse pulling it. It is coming
this way. Of all things!"

His shouts brought Grandmother to the
door.

Now it is hard to believe, but when
Grandmother looked, there really was a
little white house with a red roof coming
down the long white road.

"I wonder if someone lives in it and where it is going," shouted Paddy.

The little house came nearer.

"I can see a man sitting at the front door," Paddy went on. "He is old. I can tell he is. He has white hair and white whiskers. And look! He is stopping his house right at the end of our fence."

Paddy jumped down from the umbrella tree and raced out of the gate. In a minute he was standing by the side of the house on wheels.

"Howdy, my boy," said the man, who sat smoking his pipe. "How do you like my shop?"

"Oh! Is it a shop?" asked Paddy.

"Don't tell me a big boy like you can't read," said the man.

The man pointed to the other side of the house on wheels and Paddy ran around in a hurry to see what was on it.

Painted in big red letters was

HANDY JOE'S SHOP

"Well, did you ever?" said Paddy. "What do you sell?"

"Everything in there," the man answered, "but I'm not going to open up until I get my horse some water. Do you think I can get water at your well?"

"Come right this way," said Paddy.

Then Grandmother and Grandfather came out to the well and began to talk to Joe.

Paddy was wishing that Joe would show him his shop. Joe was wishing that Grandmother would ask him to supper.

"Supper smells good this time of day," Joe said. "I smelled it away down the road."

"Better stop and eat with us," said Grandmother. "Hot biscuits and chicken —what do you think about that?"

"I surely think I'm lucky," said Joe.

Paddy thought supper would never be over. Joe talked about everything, but most of all about Grandmother's biscuits.

"Never tasted better in my life," Joe said every time the biscuits came around.

He cut each biscuit in two, put on some yellow butter and some red, red jelly, and away that biscuit went.

At last the biscuits were all gone. But Grandmother had something else just as good as the biscuits—a big banana pie.

Of course, Joe had to have one piece and then another. For once Paddy wished that Grandmother's suppers were not so good.

But all things end at last.

"Guess I'll have to open up my shop before dark," Joe said, as he got up from the table.

Paddy's eyes just danced. He was so delighted.

Joe went around to the front of the house, pulled some ropes, and the side that had the sign, "Handy Joe's Shop," went right up into the air.

Inside was one shelf after another, and every shelf was full of something. There were rings and bracelets. There were pots and pans, men's caps, bird cages, blankets, dishes, and toys. There were boxes of this and bottles of that.

But why try to tell all that Joe had in his shop. You would never believe a shop could hold so much.

The thing Paddy would never forget was a wonderful watch that could tell time in the dark. Joe let Paddy put it on his arm and run to a dark corner of the barn to see for himself.

"Do you sell watches like this, Joe?" he asked when he came back.

"For four dollars apiece," said Joe. "Why not save your money and buy one? I'll be back this way late this summer."

Then Joe said he must be on his way. He took a pretty yellow bowl out of his shop and gave it to Grandmother.

"I just want to give you this," he said, "to pay for that good supper.

"Do you know," he went on, as he climbed up to his seat, "in all my life I have never seen the ocean. Someday I am going to take a ship to South America. Now I'm going for a summer's rest on the sandy seashore. Good-by, everyone."

And Handy Joe's Shop rolled on to the next town, ten miles away.

Money to Save

The next day Paddy had to go to the store for Grandmother. All the way down the long road, he tried to think how he could earn money to buy that watch.

It was a lucky thing for Paddy that the road ran along the edge of the woods. There were blackberries in the woods — big juicy blackberries.

The minute Paddy saw the berries, he thought, "I'll pick blackberries and sell them. I'll begin picking just as soon as I come back from the store."

"Pick me! Pick me!" the blackberries seemed to say when Paddy went into the woods.

And that is just what Paddy did. He picked a big pail full. Then he took the pail over to Mrs. Small, who lived away back off the road. She gave Paddy ten cents for his pail of berries.

"Come every day," said Mrs. Small. "Some days I'll want two pails full."

By the end of the week Paddy had almost a dollar in his bank.

Then something happened.

Trouble for Paddy

One day Paddy ran over to Mrs. Small's with his pail of berries. He rang the bell, but no one came to the door. He ran around to the back door and called. There was no one at home.

"I'll come back tomorrow," thought Paddy. "But the berries won't be so good then. Maybe I can sell them at the store."

But the storekeeper had too many berries already. He did not want any more.

Then Paddy tried everywhere, but no one would buy his berries.

As he walked along, old Granny West called to him, "Howdy, Paddy! Isn't this a pretty day?"

"Do you want some berries?" asked Paddy.

"Nothing I should like more. I haven't tasted one this year. They do tell me the woods are full of berries, but I can't get out to pick them. Now maybe I can make some jelly."

Granny West was a good friend of Paddy's, so he had to tell her all his troubles. Of course, Granny listened.

"I can't find anyone to buy my berries. I just can't," he said over and over. "How will I ever get that watch?"

"I'm sorry that I can't give you some money for your berries. Maybe sometime I can do something for you. You know I would now, if I could," said Granny.

Next day it was the same. There were berries enough but no one to buy them. Mrs. Small was still away from home.

Paddy hoped each day that someone would buy his berries. But he could only sell a few, and Granny West got more and more. Before long she had shelf after shelf full of jelly.

"I couldn't eat it all if I lived to be a hundred and ate nothing else," she said, as she shook her head.

Granny tried to help Paddy think of a way to make money, but she just couldn't.

Days went by and all the blackberries in the woods were gone. Paddy gave up trying to sell anything. He tried to forget about the watch, too.

Handy Joe Again

One day in late summer, Paddy was seated high in the chinaberry tree. He was looking over the hills and far away and wishing that something exciting would come down the long white road.

All at once he made a discovery. There, just as before, was a house on wheels coming down the long white road.

"Why, of all things!" shouted Paddy. "It is Joe and he is stopping at Granny West's house. She can't buy anything. He won't stay long there."

Maybe Granny could not buy anything, but Joe did stay a long time—long enough for Grandmother to make biscuits.

Even then he did not come, and in the end Grandmother had to send Paddy down to Granny's house after him.

Again Joe talked and talked. Again he said that Grandmother's biscuits were the best he had ever tasted. Brown biscuits, yellow butter, red, red jelly, and away they went—one after another.

Again Paddy listened and waited and wished that Grandmother's suppers were not so good.

At last supper was over and they all went out to the shop. There were so many things to look at that they did not see someone coming down the road.

All at once she stood there—old Granny West with her cane.

"Howdy everyone," she said. Her voice sounded happy and her smile was good to see.

"Long time since I came to see you," she went on. "I forgot something when Joe was at my house. I want a watch that tells time in the dark."

They all turned to look at Granny as if they thought she did not know what she was talking about—I mean, all but Joe. He was looking for the watch.

"Why, Granny West," said Grandfather. "What do you want with a watch?"

"Just one of my little jokes! Been wanting one all summer," said Granny, as she took out the money to pay for it.

"Where did you get so much money?" asked Grandmother.

"I just sold Joe 'most all the jelly I made this summer, and I want this watch for the boy who helped me," said Granny, as she handed the watch to Paddy. How proud she looked!

"Oh! Thank you! Thank you!" he said.

"Joe says he can sell all the jelly I gave him," Granny went on, "and I still have some left for winter. I never have had so much fun in one summer since I grew up, and I could not have done a thing if it had not been for Paddy."

"Did you ever?" said Paddy, as he looked at his watch. "Did you ever?"

"No, I never," said Grandfather. "No, I never."

COBBLER JIM

Friends Together

It was morning in Friendly Village—a morning in the late summertime. Down on the street that ran along the river, the door of the little brown cobbler shop opened. Then a voice from within called:

"Here, Joe! Where are you, Old Man? Always trotting off somewhere you don't belong! Come here, you rascal! Come here!"

Then down the street came a big black cat, running as fast as a cat can run. And out of the door of the cobbler shop came Cobbler Jim. He was almost as old and brown as the shoes he mended.

"You old rascal," he said. "You old rascal."

But the black cat must have been the kind of a rascal the old cobbler liked, because he leaned right over, picked him up, and put him on his shoulder, saying, "Here we are again. The old man and his cat. How are you, Old Fellow?"

You could tell by the way the cat purred and the old cobbler looked at him that they understood each other.

"Summer is about over," the cobbler said, as he looked about him. "A good many summers have come and gone since first I came to Friendly Village. But I have never had such a lonesome one."

"There is a lazy feeling in the air this morning, Joe," he went on. "I'm glad I haven't much work to do. But little as there is, I had better be about it."

Cobbler Jim walked into the shop with Joe on his shoulder. As he sat down at his workbench, the black cat jumped to the floor and went to sleep at his feet.

"One pair to mend and I'm through," the cobbler said. He whistled as he picked up an old shoe and cut off the sole.

"Run-down heels and holes in the soles! Where you have been to, no one knows. But I can't have you looking like this," he said, as he looked at the shoe.

Old Shoes to Mend

The clock ticked, the cobbler whistled, the cat purred, and the minutes flew by.

"Mended at last! Away with you," said Cobbler Jim, and the first shoe took its place on the shelf.

He had just started on the next shoe when the bell over the shop door rang and rang.

There in the doorway stood Bobby and Billy, looking as alike as twins could look. And each one had a pair of old shoes in his hand.

"Well I declare," said Cobbler Jim, looking up from his work. "Things will begin moving in this town now. When did you two mischief-makers get home?"

"Just last night," said Billy, "and our shoes are full of holes. Mother wants you to mend them and shine them, too. Can you mend them while we wait?"

"Upon my word! You two have forgotten how to read. Run out and look at the sign over my door."

"We know what it says," said Bobby. "Shoes Mended While You Wait."

"Well, that's what it means then," said Cobbler Jim, as he held up one of Bobby's shoes to look at the hole in the sole.

As he did so, some sand fell right out of the shoe onto the workbench.

"Not hard to tell where you two have been for the summer. To the seashore, I declare."

"That is right," said Bobby and Billy.

Then while Billy sat cross-legged on one side of Mr. Jim and Bobby sat cross-legged on the other, they told him all the things that had happened that summer.

Ting-a-ling! The bell over the shop door rang again, and there in the door stood a cowboy. No, it was not a cowboy after all. It was only Jack dressed in his cowboy suit.

"Well, so you are back again?" said Mr. Jim, and his hammer stopped its tapping.

"Just for a while. Just for the winter," said Jack. "Next summer I'm going right out West again."

Jack had some shoes to be mended, too.
There was no place for him on the seat
with Mr. Jim, but there was a place for
him on one corner of the workbench and
there he sat.

For the next few minutes the shop was
full of stories of cowboys and Indians,
crabs and clams, captains and monkeys.
All Mr. Jim could do was hammer away
and say, "Is that so?" once in a while.

The sun was shining through the open
door of the shop and falling on the workbench where Mr. Jim was at work.

All at once the sun did not shine on
the workbench because something big was
standing in the door and keeping the sun
out.

It was Mr. Carl with an old shoe under
each arm and his hands in his pockets.
He was standing on the step outside looking up at the sign over the door.

There was a big smile on his face as
he walked into the shop.

"Shoes mended while you wait—that is, if you wait long enough," said Mr. Carl, as he sat down on the other end of the workbench.

"Yes, and you will have a long wait this morning. Just look at all these shoes," said Cobbler Jim, as he pointed to the shoes on the workbench before him. "How are you anyway, and when did you get back from the mountains?"

"About a week ago," said Mr. Carl. Then he started in right away to tell about Lem and his fiddle and the summer in the mountains.

Tap, tap, tap went Mr. Jim's hammer. He didn't even try to say, "Is that so?" any more. He just took out his pipe and smoked and went on about his work.

"Hello, Mr. Jim. Can you mend my shoes by twelve o'clock?" someone called.

Paddy stood in the door with a pair of old shoes in his hand. Alice and Jerry were with him. Paddy had a watch on his arm and he was looking at it in a very important way.

"Well, I declare!" said Mr. Jim. "Must all the shoes in this town be mended this morning? Come here, Paddy, and let me look at that watch!"

"Look, Mr. Jim! It is very handy. It can tell time in the dark," said Paddy, as he ran over into a dark corner.

"Where did you get it," asked Mr. Carl, "and where have you been anyway? You have been gone almost three months— ever since last June."

So Paddy had to tell all about Grandmother's house with the rosebush growing
over the door, about the chinaberry tree
that looked like a big umbrella, and about
Handy Joe and the things he sold.

Then he told them how Granny West
made jelly out of his juicy blackberries.

"Picking blackberries is all right if you
can sell them after you pick them," said
Paddy. "Anyway, I liked Granny. She
was old—almost a hundred, I guess—and
she had to walk with a cane. I used to
help her. She never said, 'Hello.' She
always said, 'Howdy,' and I liked that."

When Paddy was all through talking, he wanted to know what everyone else had been doing. So the stories started all over again. How interested everyone was!

But do you know? When Alice and Jerry told about the day Dolly joined the circus and about the old bicycle in the barn and about the goat, everyone thought that Alice and Jerry had had the most fun of all, even if they had stayed at home.

"I'm not sorry they did," said Mr. Jim. "Their shoes are mended. That is a lucky thing for me on a morning like this."

The clock ticked, the hammer tapped, and soon it was twelve o'clock.

"I smell biscuits baking," said Mr. Carl at last. "Surely it isn't dinnertime already. Upon my word, it is. Time for me to be getting home for some biscuits and butter of my own."

Then everyone else remembered that he was hungry, too.

Bobby's and Billy's shoes were mended, but the other shoes were still on Mr. Jim's workbench.

"The rest of you will have to come back this afternoon," said Mr. Jim. "There is no other way out of it. I couldn't mend all these shoes in one morning—not to save my life, I couldn't. How could I work fast anyway with all this talking?"

Everyone went away laughing and talking and calling, "Good-by."

Mr. Jim got up from his workbench for the first time that morning, calling, "Here, Joe! Where are you, Old Man? Come here, you rascal, come here."

The cobbler stood for a minute in the door of his shop.

Then down the street came a big black cat running as fast as a cat can run.

Mr. Jim leaned down, picked him up, and put him on his shoulder.

"Did I say there was a lazy feeling in the air, Joe, and not much work to be done? I didn't know what I was talking about, Old Fellow. I didn't know what I was talking about. Come on! We want some dinner, too."

Acknowledgments

Grateful acknowledgment is made to the following authors and publisher for special permission to make adaptations from copyrighted materials:

Margery Bianco for "Dolly Joins the Circus."

Ellis Credle for "Pig-a-Wee."

Mrs. G. W. Trumbull for "Did You Ever."

Estelle Urbahns for "Singing Boy" from *The Courage of Singing Boy.*

Doubleday, Doran and Co., Inc., for "Blueberry Pie" from *Peter Pocket's Luck* by May Justus.

Word List

The following list includes 387 words in this *Second Reader* that were not taught in the *Basic Primer* and the *First Reader*. Of these, 86% are in the Gates list and 96% are in the Thorndike list. Of the 387 words, 69 (marked *) will not be new to pupils who have read the *Readiness Second Reader, Down the River Road.*

Since the suffixes s, es, d, ed, er, est, ing, y, and ly have been treated in the *First* and *Second Reader Companion Books* and in the *Teacher's Guidebooks* for the first and second years, a word with one of these endings is not considered new in the *Second Reader* after the basic form of the word has been taught. All derived forms are counted as new until the basic form has been introduced. Compound words, whether hyphenated or not, are not considered new if both parts of the word have been taught.

Presentation Unit			
0 stories	5 exciting* happen* even*	9 such* didn't	13 shoe*
1 friendly village live*	6 joins circus	10 an* clown	14 black- smith shop end
2 through* side*	7 fruit* horse	11 suppose* spending baseball*	15 music ears* trot*
3	8 gray blind eye*	12 gone* course tell*	16 acting hold* nothing*
4 friends*			

17 dancing
 began*
 step*

18 laugh
 shout*
 stood*

19 tents*

20

21 rode*
 minute*

22 afternoon*
 almost*
 last*

23 bought
 bottles

24 ever*
 throw*
 done*

25 full*
 left*

26 clean
 threw
 noise*

27 story*
 sure
 second*

28 ladder

29 worms*
 don't*

30 less
 than*
 shiver

31 won't*
 think*

32 bicycle
 wheel*
 rest

33 might*
 dark*
 corner*

34 hard

35 them-
 selves*
 fall*
 pieces*

36 lucky*
 found*

Absorption Unit

37 feeling*
 bones*

38 seven
 o'clock
 feel

39 kitchen
 believe

40

41 only*
 place

42 missed

43 eight
 Mrs.
 should

44 seen
 cellar

45

46 told*
 upset

47

48

49

50

51 since

52

53 mischief

54

55

56 crowd
 middle

57 grass

58 better*
 remem-
 bered*
 seem

59

60 cents
 tired*
 under-
 stand

61

62

63

64

65 mountain

Presentation Unit

66 deep
 pine

67 log
 cabin
 trails

68 hollows
 own
 Lem

69 lonesome
 horn
 morning-
 glory

70 rope
 Granny
 Preacher

71 skinny
 piglets

72 melon
 patch

73

74 under
 fence*
 potato

75 smoke
 chimney
 smell*

76 fireplace
 pots
 pans*

77 root
 herself

78 edge
 wondered

79 proudly
   fine*

80 wait

81

82 wonderful
   corn

83 blueberry
   pie
   juice

84 bowl
   bread
   dinner

85 yellow
   pup
   whistle

86 floor
   fault

87 rich
   supper

88 peddler
   golden

89 fire*
   bark*

90 let

91 shiny
   hurt
   buy*

92

93

94 nice
   enjoy
   myself

95

96

Absorption Unit

97 fiddle

98 floats
   foot
   guess

99 berries

100 air

101

102 Charlie
    learn

103 keep

104 foolish

105

106 our

107 bee
    miles

108

109 prize

110

111 bacon

112

Presentation Unit

113 Indians

114 great
    plains
    rolling

115 cattle
    grazing

116 leaf
    pasture

117 bang
    stand
    hair

118 West
    Uncle

119 can't
    watch

120 slept

121 most
    these
    ranch

122 declare
    fellow

123 question
    suit*

124 hot
    clouds

125 low
    feet
    corral

126 slid
    real
    I'm

127 cook

128 mouth
    song
    range

129

130 mine

131 dressed
    hurry

132 graze

133 glad

134 which
    I'll

135 ask

136

137 careful
    flapjacks

138 twirled
    try
    small

139 trouble
    tied
    saddle

140 forgotten
    begin

141 Navaho
    silver

142 rings
    blankets
    sheep

143 hogan
    grown
    family

144 feast

145 food

146 filled
    high

147 drove
    dance
    camp

148 race
    win
    dollar*

9 8 1   F.W.